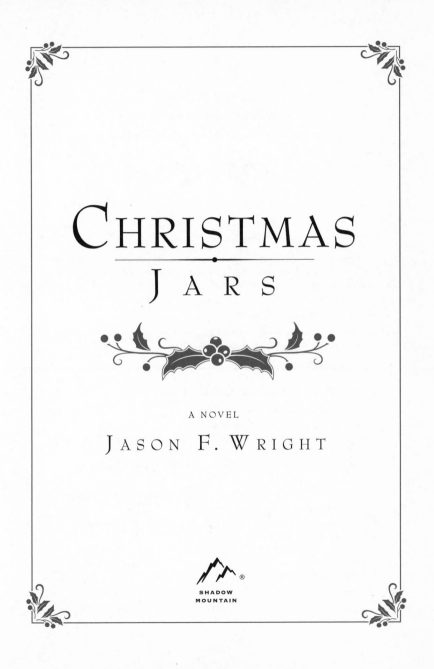

CHRISTMAS
JARS

A NOVEL

JASON F. WRIGHT

SHADOW
MOUNTAIN

For my children
Oakli Shane, Jadi Thompson,
Kason Samuel, and Koleson Ward

Library of Congress Cataloging-in-Publication Data

Names: Wright, Jason F., author.
Title: Christmas jars / Jason F. Wright.
Description: Collector's edition. | Salt Lake City, Utah : Shadow Mountain, [2017]
Identifiers: LCCN 2017012063 | ISBN 9781629723297 (hardbound : alk. paper)
Subjects: LCSH: Women journalists—Fiction. | Generosity—Fiction. | Christmas stories.
Classification: LCC PS3623.R539 C484 2017 | DDC 813/.6—dc23
LC record available at https://lccn.loc.gov/2017012063

Printed in China
RR Donnelley, Shenzhen, China

10   9   8   7   6   5   4   3   2   1

LETTER FROM THE AUTHOR

It's been more than a decade since the first Christmas Jar landed on someone's doorstep. Who knew that a simple jar of coins given away on a crisp Christmas Eve would lead to this little novella? Even more surprisingly, who knew that the book would lead to a movement?

Since that first ding-dong ditch delivery, we estimate that the global Christmas Jars family has given away nearly $10 million in clean quarters and dirty dimes.

That's a lot of couch-cushion and cupholder change.

My career has changed too. After all those promises I made to my teachers, mother, wife, and God that I'd become a writer when I grew up—I finally grew up.

I've written eleven more books with several more in the literary oven. I've written biographies, dabbled in ghostwriting, and been published in newspapers, magazines, and on websites across the country.

Of course I love my regular column with *Fox News*, the *Deseret News*, and my hometown paper, the fantastic *Northern Virginia Daily*.

Admittedly, some of the writing has hit the mark and some hasn't. I've had hits, flops, and everything in between. But I keep putting words to paper because I cling to hope there's one reader who needs the right message at the right moment.

The book that won't quit also launched a speaking career. I've been blessed beyond measure to speak to corporate, church, and nonprofit groups large and small in nearly every state. I've also presented assemblies and workshops to hundreds of thousands of K-12 students.

Confession? My favorite part of being a writer isn't the writing. It's looking in the dreaming eyes of a young student and telling them that no matter what life throws their way, I will always believe in them.

Because that's exactly what my teachers said to me.

Films are coming, too. Under my new company of the same name, my loyal investors and I are developing several projects in the *Christmas Jars* brand for film and television. Also watch for some short films based on the best of the real-life Christmas Jar miracles.

Still, despite all this, we know that nothing will replace the magic of the Christmas Jar movement.

During the first few years after its publication, I wondered if I'd ever be known for anything other than the little novella someone once teased me was so short it should have been shelved in the pamphlet aisle.

Even now, at every stop, every signing, and in every interview, I'm asked about the really little book with really long legs. Recently, an independent bookstore owner asked me at the end of an event if it bothered me that *Christmas Jars* is still my most popular book.

Countless coins and miracles later, I humbly answer, "Not at all. What a blessing."

Indeed. What a miracle that a book born from a family experiment has turned into a tradition that changes lives and answers prayers.

Plus, as my wise wife once told me, this story and tradition doesn't belong to me anyway. It never has.

It belongs to every single person who has been touched by the magic of a jar.

It's miraculous, isn't it? A tiny tradition in our

small family has grown into a massive movement in a global family that will never stop growing.

I hope you'll join us.

PS: This gorgeous Collector's Edition, like every other printing before it, is the work of a team unparalleled in publishing. They are Sheri Dew, Jeff Simpson, Laurel Christensen Day, David Brown, Chris Schoebinger, Heidi Taylor Gordon, Lisa Mangum, Derk Koldewyn, Richard Erickson, Malina Grigg, and Sheryl Dickert Smith. Thanks also to my Christmas Jars business partners: Aaron and Jessica Blight, Bruce and Tamara Brubaker, David Goodwin, Michael and Tanya Groll, Dale Jensen, Rickie and Karyn Killinger, Billy Lynch, John and Trena Moore, Dan and Patricia Utley, and Catherine Minor Worley. Finally, love and gratitude to my most important partner of all—my wonderful wife, Kodi Erekson Wright. I love you.

For more information or to share your
Christmas Jar miracle, visit www.christmasjars.com.

For more information about the author,
visit www.jasonfwright.com.

PROLOGUE

Introducing Hope

Louise Jensen was sitting alone, licking her fingers two at a time and paying serious attention to her greasy chicken-leg-and-thigh platter, when she heard muffled crying from the booth behind her at Chuck's Chicken 'n' Biscuits on U.S. Highway 4. It was early Friday afternoon. It was also New Year's Eve.

Although discovering an unattended, blue-eyed, newborn baby girl was not on her list of expectations, Louise was the faithful brand of woman who believed that everything happened for a reason. She reached down and lifted the pinkish baby into her arms. Tucked inside a stained elephant blanket, near the baby's neck, she found an unsigned, handwritten note:

To the next person to hold my baby girl,

She is yours now. I'll miss her more than you know. But I love her too much to raise her with a daddy that hits. Truth is, he didn't even want me to have her anyways, and her life will be better without a mommy that will always need to run. Please tell her I love her. And please tell her I will hold her again.

I cannot give her much, but this year I give her the life her daddy wouldn't. And a little bit of hope.

Though a middle-aged, never-married house cleaner—and one hardly in a position to assume financial responsibility for another mouth—Louise knew this was no random moment. Every year she ate Christmas Eve dinner at Chuck's. But one week ago she'd been bedridden, caught in the throes of a punishing bout with influenza. So with a 103-degree temperature and with pained reluctance she had postponed—for the first time ever—her annual chicken dinner. The spring had returned to Louise's step the morning of the thirty-first, three full days before she'd expected, and she had ventured off to Chuck's.

Her eyes darted around the dining room at the handful of semi-strangers, and she sensed that without realizing it, the mother of this baby had somehow known that on New Year's Eve, at that very hour, Louise Jensen would finally be eating a belated but traditional Christmas Eve dinner.

She looked around at the oblivious diners, eating and chatting about grand plans for the year ahead, their faces illuminated by the glow of Chuck's overdone red and green holiday decorations. Above their heads hung silver tinsel, draped over faded lampshades, and an artificial tree guarded the door. High atop the tree, instead of a traditional star or white angel, sat a stuffed frowny-face cartoon chicken. At the cash register, Chuck's wife was changing the batteries in a boogie-dancing Santa.

Louise nestled the baby in her coat, left a ten-dollar bill on the table, and slipped out the side door. "Happy New Year, Louise!" someone called just as the door swung shut. She did a half turn and smiled back, keeping her stride and not slowing until she reached her rusty El Camino at the far end of the parking lot. She looked both ways—twice—then buckled the bundled baby into the passenger seat and rolled as slowly as the engine allowed approximately four miles to the nearest business district. She talked her way down the road, asking questions for which she feared she'd never hear the answers, and for the first time in history feeling grateful for the flu.

Born herself to a single mother, Louise made independence central to her life plan long before she took her first job babysitting for a half dozen children in her apartment complex. She was ten at the time.

A healthy appreciation of work was hardwired into a long line of Jensens. For as long as Louise could remember, her mother had worked as many as three jobs simultaneously. Her mom saved what she could, praying that one day Louise and her brother would go to college and accomplish more than she had. But Louise never imagined a life beyond what she'd lived with her mother. Her idol worked every day until her hands and back were sore, treating everyone she met like family, and burying needless criticism of others so deep beneath the soil of everyday living that only kindness ever saw the light.

While Louise's brother was away attending technical college, Louise graduated from high school and continued working right alongside her mother. Though most of her childhood friends appeared to stop growing sometime before graduation, Louise added another three inches between her eighteenth and twentieth years. She finally stopped at a barefoot six-feet tall. Her thick, dark brown hair fell down and ended at the small of her back. Her eyes were big and milk-chocolate brown—the kind no one forgets.

Louise and her mother took on restaurants, hotels, grocery stores, and even a service station or two. But what they most enjoyed was cleaning the homes of a small circle of wealthy clients. Together, they turned their two-woman maid service into an art form, cleaning every home as if it were their own.

The pair worked for affluent families. Louise and her mother soaked in the atmosphere of husbands, wives, and their usually well-behaved children living at full speed. Though on the surface they kept a professional distance, silent relationships of trust flourished, and they learned to love and admire the good people they cleaned up after.

After Louise's mother died, Louise kept right on cleaning. She never thought it odd that she felt closest to her mother, friend, and business partner when tackling dust bunnies or when on her knees scrubbing linoleum floors.

Louise was in love with the fussy baby girl by the time she strapped her into the brand-new infant car seat. And by the next morning she would have fought to her own death to keep her. "Possession is ninetenths," she told a social worker on the phone.

A thorough investigation produced no leads as to the identity of the mother. No one recalled seeing the baby's mother in Chuck's that night; no one had seen anything out of the ordinary; and not a soul had ever returned to ask the question one might expect: "So, who's raising my daughter?" The mother, they all reasoned, was long gone. She had moved on, and so too must the rest of them.

After months of family court hearings, interviews, surprise spot-check home visits, and stacks of red tape, the state finally admitted what Louise and her small circle of friends had known all along: she would make a perfectly suitable mother. Not only that, the court ruled, but Louise Jensen represented the baby's best chance for a good life. Not that it mattered what the court said; Louise wouldn't have given her up anyway.

Driving away from what she prayed was her last visit to a courthouse, Louise looked in the rearview mirror at the child she'd known only as "baby."

"We're family now," Louise said aloud. "What should we call you?"

She named the baby Hope.

———·———

It didn't take long for Hope Jensen to realize her mother was crazy. "But the *good* crazy," she would tell her elementary school playmates. Soon after Hope's fifth birthday, Louise sat her daughter down in their favorite booth at Chuck's and prepared to play out the scene she had rehearsed hundreds of times in front of the bathroom mirror. As Hope played tic-tac-toe with hot tater tots, her mother shared the handwritten note and the unvarnished truth behind their first meeting. A few familiar onlookers, keenly aware of what was unfolding before them, watched with caring curiosity.

"Then you're *not* my mommy?" Hope asked during the first natural pause.

"Of course I am, sweetheart." The sensation of tears in Louise's eyes was not a familiar one. "Hope Jensen, I am every bit your mother today as I was yesterday. And the same goes for tomorrow, and all the tomorrows after that."

Hope nodded her head as if this were just another piece of the colorful mosaic they painted together. "Will we ever see her again?" Hope asked.

"I don't know, sugar," Louise answered. "But I bet she'd like to see you one day." She reached across the table and placed Hope's innocent hands in her own. "You know what? It sure couldn't have been easy saying good-bye to one of God's most special little girls."

Hope sat quietly, processing the unfolding news,

balancing sweetener packets on the end of a saltshaker. "Did she love me?"

"Of course she did, sugar," answered Louise. "She loved you *so* much, she gave you a better life."

Louise's concern for her daughter dissolved with the very next question.

"Okay, Mom. So can I get a limeade now?"

ONE

On her last day of kindergarten, Hope Jensen announced, walking hand in hand with her mother, that she had *finally* made a decision about her career. "One day I will grow up to become either president of the United States *or* a famous newspaper reporter."

"The latter is more honorable," her mother teased.

Hope agreed and eventually set her sights on the newsroom.

Everyone who knew her suspected that Hope began writing in the womb. As a baby, paper and pencils were in her hands more than rattles and teething biscuits. By the second grade, she was writing a series of plays about a friendly gang of motorcycle-riding bunnies. In the third grade she wrote a heart-wrenching short story about a homeless mouse that saved his family by winning the state lottery. During the fourth and fifth grades she wrote a one-page family newsletter called the *Jensen Report*. And as a gangly sixth-grader, Hope compiled an impressive list of addresses for all sorts of distant cousins, teachers, former teachers, and some people they later learned they had no relationship with at all. A four-page spread was mailed every other Monday to forty subscribers in six states plus Canada.

Hope grew into a striking-looking young woman. Through the years, her once-baby blue eyes had added a rich green at their edges. "Those aren't eyes," Louise told her, "they're jewels." Her often-pony-tailed hair was darker than most would have expected for such light eyes and fair skin.

Hope often thought of the mysterious woman who had left her in the booth at Chuck's. "Mom, do you think she still lives around here? Does she look like me? Do you think she likes pink lemonade more than yellow, like me? Does she ever think of me?"

"It just might be." It became Louise's default answer to most of the impossible questions. Hope's heart believed that one day she would get real answers, but her head told her otherwise.

Beginning on her second Christmas Eve, and every Christmas Eve thereafter, Hope and Louise Jensen kept the tradition alive by eating an early dinner at Chuck's. The meal was always the same: chicken, biscuits with real butter, and free pie with all the vanilla ice cream they could eat. They took slow and deliberate bites, telling stories and sharing visions of what lay ahead.

"You never know," Hope would tell her mother more than once as the third hour approached. "This could be the year."

"It just might be," her mother answered. But the mystery woman never came.

"Next year," Hope said, as if it were a matter of proven fact. "I just know it!"

———·———

"The precocious one," as her mother's friends liked to call Hope, became the first underclassman to be named editor-in-chief of the school paper during her sophomore year of high school. Assigning stories, editing, and selling newspaper advertising was fine, but it was writing the stories that provided the hook. "I think she bleeds ink," her mother beamed.

Hope's crowning moment, as high school faded into yearbook memories, was a feature article about the senior class career counselor who would die without a costly liver transplant. The student body raised almost nineteen thousand dollars. The counselor lived, and Hope's poignant story tied for first place in a nation-wide, high-school journalism contest.

To earn extra credit, and because she already knew how she planned to earn her real paychecks, Hope applied for and was awarded an internship at the *Daily Record*. It was the only serious newspaper in four surrounding towns. She did whatever was asked, mastering everything from the bottled water dispenser to the copy and mail-metering machines. Just two weeks after graduation she was offered a paid position.

Hope's first stop was a tiny cubicle in Classifieds. "It's a start," she told her mother the night they photocopied and framed her very first paycheck. Hope the wunderkind was on her road to a Pulitzer Prize and aimed to be the next great American journalist. Headshots of her idols—Bernstein, Woodward, and Graham—formed a square on the wall above her desk. The fourth frame that completed the square contained no photo. Instead, taped under the glass was a white piece of copy paper with the words "I'M NEXT," written in thick block letters in black marker.

Her job required just twenty-eight hours a week and offered plenty of downtime to take classes at the community college. When people called the paper, the voice on the other end of the phone belonged to the energetic eighteen-year-old writing the best ads twenty-nine dollars a week could buy. "Hottest House on the Block!" "This Candy Apple Firebird Is a Head Turner!" Nobody wrote them like Hope.

After a year of writing ads and pushing the latest "this week only" special, she was promoted to the community page, where she wrote scintillating stories on upcoming fall carnivals, book fairs, and firehouse bake sales. "I could write this stuff in my sleep," she told her mother.

"Patience, my dear. Patience."

Another eighteen months of hard work, plus year-round school, and Hope was in her final term in the journalism program. "It's time for more," she told her boss. Before her next payday she was promoted once again, this time to the editorial page. She surprised her mother with the news over takeout.

"You're a wonder," Louise said. "I am *so* proud of you."

They finished their tacos and chips as Hope fantasized aloud of the accomplishments to come. "I'll write a feature, I just know I will, and it will land on A1, *the front page!* They call that *above the fold,* Mom."

"I didn't know—"

"And of course it'll win Story of the Year. And you just know I'll be writing for the *Washington Post* before the plaque even arrives."

They ate every visible chip crumb, no matter how small, even licking their fingers to pull the final tiny shards up and onto their tongues. After they'd discarded their tinfoil wrappings and paper bags, Louise beckoned her high-flying daughter to the couch for some important news of her own. The words were as simple and stunning as Hope had ever heard.

"I have cancer."

Louise held her sobbing daughter on the couch until dawn.

TWO

The devastating reality of Louise's ovarian cancer was assuaged in time by Hope's delight at her new position. Hope's responsibilities included occasional one-on-one briefings from one of several senior editors. They spelled out the newspaper's position on important political issues, and, armed with a framework for why the paper leaned one way or another, Hope was tasked with punching out first drafts of political editorials. "The Paper Endorses George A. Lee for Governor." "The Paper Calls for a Full Investigation of Mayor Caren Floresca." "The Paper Supports the Aggressive Methods of Sheriff Eugene Jones." Hope spent hours massaging her four hundred words, only to see them slashed down by someone upstairs. But Hope wanted to work upstairs, too. *I belong upstairs,* she convinced herself.

For months Hope toiled away, and, in time, more of her own words made the printed page. Six times her editorials ran untouched. Her mother had each professionally framed. They filled a wall in their cozy apartment.

Persistent pain forced Louise to stop working not long after her diagnosis. She bade farewell to her clients and reluctantly sold her cleaning contracts to a company that had what seemed like an army of bright white-and-blue cars with "Clean Police" splattered in neon paint on both sides. Hope never fully understood why cleaning up other people's messes brought her mother such satisfaction. And though she had no idea how her modest income would support them both for long, she felt relief the first day Louise didn't head off to care for someone else's home. "You're all mine now," Hope told her.

Each morning Hope made two servings of oatmeal topped with blueberries, always blueberries, and kissed her mother good-bye. During Hope's daily absence, Louise spent hours creating elaborate pages for their near-endless library of scrapbooks. Evenings were spent reading aloud to one another or playing a specialized Jensen family version of Rummy. Hope loved the evenings.

Saturdays often included very short shopping trips downtown or a quick lunch at Chuck's. "Should we go cruisin' for boys?" Hope teased on the way home late one afternoon.

"Not this week, sweetie, maybe next."

"Ah, now. One of these days we got to find you a man, Momma!" Hope's voice twanged to her mother's delight.

"Next week, remind me, and maybe I'll wear some makeup."

Hope turned to her mother. "Miss Louise Jensen, some women don't need makeup." She tickled her mother's knee. "You couldn't get more beautiful if you swallowed last month's edition of *Cosmo*."

———·———

Because Louise's cancer was not detected earlier, her disease was well advanced by the time doctors finally diagnosed it. After unsuccessfully experimenting with less-invasive treatments, Louise relented and scheduled the surgery her doctors long insisted was her best chance. Hope was at her bedside when she finally awoke, twelve hours after bidding good-bye at the patients-only elevator.

"Hello there," Hope said, holding one of her mother's hands with both of her own.

"You're here," her mother's voice cracked.

"Of course I am, crazy woman."

"The *good* crazy?" Louise struggled to whisper.

"Yes, Mom, the *good* crazy. Now, shhh."

Louise breathed heavily. "How did we do?"

"The news is not good." Hope paused. "They say you'll never have any children of your own."

A pained chuckle turned to a cough, and Hope gently put a straw between her mother's lips. Louise took a long drink and reopened her eyes. "I *have* a child of my own." She smiled as broadly as her face allowed.

THREE

Having no idea what day Hope was actually born, Louise was allowed to choose—within reason—her daughter's birthday for the state birth certificate. She chose January first, believing the date, like her name, emblematized new chances and new beginnings. On her twenty-third such birthday, Hope sat beside her mother in an oversized recliner in their living room. She ripped open a delicately wrapped self-help book from her mother. "You know if I actually took the time to read all these books I'd have to quit my job, right, Mom?"

"Hope! Show some—"

"Gratitude! I know," she interrupted. "Oh, you know I *loovve* your books. It's just that I love *you* more." From just six inches away she blew her mother a kiss and returned with zeal to her second piece of carrot cake.

That was the last birthday Louise and Hope Jensen celebrated together. Fifty-one weeks later, though in unspeakable pain and in spite of everyone's best efforts to convince her otherwise, Louise insisted on their traditional dinner at Chuck's. They sat on the same side of the only booth they'd ever known. Louise sat on two hospital pillows, with three thin blankets draping her frail shoulders. Chuck, his wife, plus a handful of other regulars surrounded them, wishing the Jensens a happy holiday and pretending it was just another Christmas Eve. For the last time, Hope and Louise played tic-tac-toe with cooling tater tots.

Four days later Louise Jensen passed on more peacefully than even Hope could have prayed for. Lying on the couch, she rested her head on her daughter's lap, comfortably atop her favorite Christmas pillow. Hour after hour, Hope spoke in reverent whispers—at times her voice barely brushing the air—sharing stories from their years of a truly unique sisterhood. The pastel dawn sky cast healthy tones on Louise's once pale face.

Hope ran her hand over her mother's thin, sparse hair and marveled at how beautiful—even in death—her heroic mother looked.

"It's all right, Mother," Hope said, wiping a fallen tear from her own eyes across her mother's wrinkled chin. "Go." Their souls bid silent farewells, the ever-slowing rhythm of Louise's fragile chest ceased, and Hope watched her mother slip painlessly from one side of the veil to the next.

For the first time in many sore months, Hope smiled at the face of the vibrant woman who had rescued her one lifetime ago at Chuck's Chicken 'n' Biscuits.

———·———

Two weeks of overdue vacation, her boss reasoned, was exactly what Hope needed to recharge. But after just three days of sweatpants and talk shows, she'd had enough grieving. *Life has taken my mother,* she thought, *but it cannot take my collection of words.*

On Monday, Hope returned to her desk, which was still covered with a thin, pencil-yellow rubber mat, and reminded herself that the desks upstairs had leather. The waiting game was over. *It's time to move.*

"Good morning, Mr. Butler!" So began the campaign for her promotion upstairs.

"Morning, kid," the mid-sixties man answered.

"Actually, it's Hope."

"Good to see you." He talked as he moved through a tight pattern of cheap desks toward the staircase at the back of the sports department bullpen. "Your first day?"

"What? No. No, Mr. Butler, I've been here a while. I write some of the drafts for the paper's opinion page."

"Oh, yes, good, then." He was halfway up the stairs now. "Enjoy Monday."

"You, too! Enjoy!" She would've sucked the words back in if she could have. *Good grief,* she thought, *my schmooze needs a tune-up.*

Hope honed her writing and punched out some of the most crisp, colorful editorials the paper had ever seen. At every opportunity she peppered her new friend, Lyle Butler, with questions on the industry, writing, and getting ahead. Appreciative of her energy and zest, he introduced her to the other senior editors, the department heads, and even the classifieds manager, someone she'd previously worked with for almost six months. Through it all, Lyle recognized enormous talent in the former intern.

Then came the call. "Can you come up?"

"I'm halfway there." Hope fast-walked from her desk downstairs through the mouse maze and up the staircase.

He wasted no time. "You ready to move your things?"

"Where to, Boss?"

"Up the stairs to a full-size editorial desk. Still an associate, of course, but out of the trap down there." He gestured out his window to the floor below.

"I'll be right back." She was fully prepped to say her good-byes and fill her arms with everything she could in one trip and climb back up the stairs before someone changed his mind.

"Take your time, kid. Your desk up here is safe."

Hope spent five minutes chatting with a few people, packed her personal items, stuck a pencil sharpener that she'd adopted a year before into her bag, and walked slowly—very slowly—back across the first floor. She thought she heard a few scattered "Congrats, Hope," but they were probably imagined.

Hope knew that first trip up the stairs was a seminal moment custom-made for one of her mother's thick scrapbooks. Hope put one foot in front of the other, eyes partially closed, her mind successfully canceling most of the ambient noise from the bustle below. Beneath eyes wet with unfinished grief, she struggled to hear the whispered voice of her mother. "I *knew* you could do it," Hope thought she heard Louise say.

"Thanks, Mom," she mouthed back.

Hope was soon writing most of the newspaper's political editorials, with rarely significant edits from her colleagues upstairs. Occasionally they disagreed over finer points, but she had earned ample trust and had a more-than-adequate leash on which to roam.

She pitched her first feature story on the growing skepticism behind global warming. Three weeks of research and interviews, and she had a three-thousand-word feature: "Global Warming: Legit Scare or Liberal Hot Air?" It was good, they told her, but not right for the front page. It ran on A9 but roused more phone calls and letters than she had ever received from her controversial recaps of local chess tournaments. For the first time, Hope tasted the success she had first craved as an eager middle school newsletter publisher. Soon her life of writing copy for page A9 would end.

One afternoon Lyle asked if Hope was ready to attend occasional newspaper business meetings. These were big-picture discussions about the direction of the paper: How could they boost circulation? How could they lure back subscribers that had fallen to the dreaded weekend-only status? What was the key to increasing ad revenues? Who would the paper endorse in the latest political horse race? She enjoyed seeing the machines behind the business of newspaper production. She marveled at the process that resulted in printed words—words that each morning just floated in the air around them but by press time had landed on a three-section, 36-page newspaper. They worked like crazed ants:

writing, editing, trimming photos, editing more, trimming ads, and squeezing every last letter out of every word plugged into every page to meet the all-important deadline. They congratulated each other with hearty pats on the back as if they had accomplished something unprecedented. Then they did it all over again the next day.

Hope pitched a handful of other front-page articles but was sanctimoniously turned down. "Not enough general interest." "We need to sell more papers." "Go find a real story." Even when she got a green light, it was usually given to another reporter, and she was assigned as editor. "You've got too much on your plate, Hope," Lyle said. "Just because you're on the team responsible for the newspaper's content doesn't mean you have to write it all."

The months on Hope's *Reader's Digest* calendar flipped by without her even having time to turn the pages. She wrote less, edited more, and learned everything imaginable about newspapers. She was asked to fine-tune her skills as a newspaperwoman, but in return her love for the stories themselves began to wane.

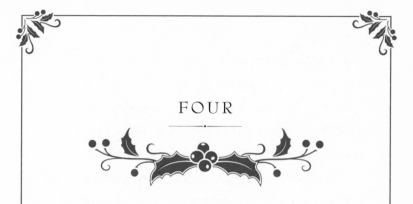

FOUR

Hope was in a blue funk that turned royal on December twenty-fourth. Sore from crying, and desperate for her mother, Hope spent her first Christmas Eve alone at Chuck's. With her first mother's goodbye note resting deep in her pocket, Hope picked at her dinner and pie and answered a thousand and one "Merry Christmas" wishes.

"This was your mom's favorite time of year," all the women said.

"Look, Hope," their husbands added, "you call us if you need anything. You hear me? You need a place to come tonight?"

Hope politely turned them all down and sat for

three hours before Chuck and his wife said it was time to go. "Do you mind if I stay a little longer?"

"Of course not." Chuck sent his wife home and found busywork in the kitchen. He would stay as long as she needed. Just after eight, Hope thanked Chuck and kissed him on the cheek, and drove home to sleep away the day's final, lonely hours. Rounding the hallway corner to her apartment door, her stride froze at the sight of her front door hanging slightly open.

"Hello!" She nudged it open another foot, yelling in the most dangerous voice she could muster. "My husband and I are home. We're coming in and we're heavily armed." She pushed the door the rest of the way open and took a single step in. "That's right, I said *heavily armed!*" She took another step in, and found a mess she previously imagined could only be caused by a south-Texas tornado.

Hope slid cautiously into the living room, breathing in short, quick bursts that synced with her racing heart. She stood motionless, moving only her eyes and surveying the wreckage. Gone were her stereo, cheap television, and two crystal horses her uncle had sent just one year back. Toppled and broken was an inexpensive fluorescent lamp she'd been meaning to replace for months.

She examined the other rooms only after convincing herself that her intruders were not lying under her couch or still hiding behind the hanging blue jeans in the bedroom closet. Kitchen and dresser drawers hung tenuously on their tracks. Missing was a wristwatch she had received as a child from her mother but never wore for fear of breaking it or worse—losing it. Also missing was five hundred dollars in emergency cash she and her mother kept hidden in an envelope in a drawer under the plastic silverware tray.

She dialed 911, and within ten minutes three police officers arrived to search her apartment. Hope, torn somewhere between tears and a tantrum she knew no one would want to witness, slipped down two flights of stairs and outside to catch her breath. She leaned against the brick building's side, eyes closed. The crisp night air cooled her cheeks, and though it would have been natural to cry, she didn't. Her thoughts turned naturally to Louise. *Ah, come on, Mother. These are the kinds of things that happen to* other *people.*

She tried to keep warm by rubbing her hands together and sticking them up her sleeves to her forearms. She counted forty-plus years that her mother had cleaned homes. *All those houses, all those families, and not a single break-in, ever? Couldn't you have left me a pinch of luck?*

Hope returned when she could no longer tolerate the steady chattering of her teeth. She stumbled over a brown sack sitting just inside the open apartment door. She picked it up and nearly dropped it on her foot; it was much heavier than it looked. She reached in and pulled out a large glass jar filled with money. It held silver change mostly, but three or four twenty-dollar bills also snaked through the tightly packed coins. She approached one of the officers. "Is this yours?"

"No, ma'am. It just showed up there. We figured it was takeout or something." The officer went back to pulling prints from the inside knob of the front door.

Hope asked the other two officers who were dutifully processing her very own personal crime scene.

All anyone could say was that it was definitely full of money, it hadn't been there a half hour before, and it was probably a gift. *Geniuses,* Hope thought.

It was still early enough that she knocked on her neighbor's doors to the left and right. They knew nothing of the jar but would happily take it if she decided she couldn't. A recent move-in across the hall, a quiet but confident single woman, also hadn't seen or heard anything but told her to enjoy it. "Use it to replace what you've lost, sweetie. Somebody was thinking of you. How lucky!"

"Merry Christmas," Hope answered, thanking her and turning back to her own front door. The police were finishing and promised to get right on "finding the perps." They mentioned four other break-ins in nearby buildings and encouraged her not to give up. "We'll catch these sick, disgusting creeps," one said, stepping out the front door with his bag full of evidence. "Merry Christmas!"

Hope shook the officers' hands, and her eyes followed them down the stairs. She stood an extra moment in her doorway, staring down, letting her eyes glaze over in imagination. She pictured a person in a rented, baggy Santa suit and fluffy beard slithering down the hallway, leaving the jar, and vanishing as quickly as he'd arrived. But it wasn't a he. The visitor wasn't stout with a sturdy frame and jolly eyes. It was a woman's figure she saw. And her eyes looked just like her mother's.

Hope shook her head quickly as if to jostle the daydream back to its place. She stepped into her apartment and shut the door behind her. In what the police estimated was only three or four minutes, Hope's uninvited holiday guests had effectively turned over her entire life. She'd never felt so robbed—not of money or possessions, but of space and security. Someone she didn't know, a criminal, maybe two, had broken in and rummaged through her very private history.

She took the jar and sat on the futon in the family room in front of where her television once sat. Rotating the jar with both hands, she noticed for the first time, in red and green, the words "Christmas Jar." They were hand-painted across the center of the eight-inch-tall clear glass jar. She dumped out the contents on the reading table, sorted the coins by type, and began counting. She twice totaled $154.76 in change and another $80 in cash. *Why? From whom?*

Hope knew this was just the sort of fabulous mystery her mother's rainbow spirit had been made for. *So I'll solve it for us both,* she thought. Her mind was already spinning theories, and her eyes settled on a photo of the two of them hanging on the wall across the room. *And then I'll write the story.*

FIVE

Hope spent most of Christmas Day at the newspaper, assuring another workaholic colleague that her break-in did not make her a high-risk kidnapping target. Together they theorized on who might have reacted with such breakneck speed and left the generous—and very bizarre—gift.

The next morning she took the jar to the bank, cashed in the change, and stopped at a hardware store to buy a small but sturdy steel personal safe. She also purchased a twelve-inch television set and stopped by an insurance office to arrange for a no-frills renter's insurance policy. Then she drove back to the newspaper, with the jar still firmly planted at the front of her never-resting mind.

That afternoon Hope was reminded of a hard deadline approaching for a series of articles on the pros and cons of an upcoming bond referendum for public financing of a new county prison complex. There was tangible pressure to make progress on at least the first of the three pieces, but nothing could pry her mind from the jar. Where had it come from? Whose money was it? Was she to spend it? Save it? Pass it on to someone more needy? Above all else, why had she been chosen? Certainly there were others, countless others, more needy than she was.

Putting the prison assignment aside, Hope searched the paper's archive database for the words *Christmas* and *Jar*. To her amazement, she found three letters to the editor in recent years that all told similarly mysterious stories. Each was, in essence, a thank-you note to some anonymous benefactor.

"My name is Kimberly Telford," the first letter began, "and I owe someone the biggest thank-you of my life. No one beyond my husband and doctor knows this, but in early December I suffered my third consecutive miscarriage."

The letter detailed the woman's depression leading up to Christmas and then the subsequent discovery of a jar full of change on her front step on December twenty-fourth. The money, almost four hundred dollars, went toward fertility treatments that her insurance company refused to cover. She and her husband had been trying unsuccessfully for five years for the baby that he believed would finally make their marriage complete. Her husband said over and over that only a baby boy would make their relationship "relevant in the eternities," as he put it. Her doctors believed the intense anxiety and stress were the primary factors preventing a viable pregnancy.

The near-nonstop fighting created uncertainty about where their lives might lead them, if anywhere at all. At her lowest, the woman realized her marriage had morphed into two single adults living together, roommates, no longer as a couple, and no longer as two people with one cause.

It was then, with her husband fast asleep in the bedroom and Kimberly's soul teetering on the brink of giving up, that a knock on the door startled her. She wiped her eyes and nose and went to her front door. At her feet was the jar, wrapped in a gold ribbon and full of cash and change. "It wasn't what I pulled from the jar that helped most," Kimberly's letter concluded. "It was what you put inside. Thank you for telling me that I am not alone. I am not alone!"

Hope's eyes rested on the last lines for an extra moment before scrolling down to the second letter.

"Some holidays are better than others," the next letter began. "But this year will be hard to top." The letter was signed by a local college student and aspiring chemist John Willard. He'd been sitting at a bus stop on Christmas Eve, when two children—eight or nine years old, he judged—handed him a jar packed to the lid with nothing but quarters. John, away from his family for the first time, was en route to the college library. "But really," the letter disclosed, "I was running from the sadness of being away from Mom and Dad and the family farm I was born on."

He took the jar, thanked the children, and smiled as they raced each other around a corner, out of sight, but forever into the rich creases of John's mind. He sat frozen on the bench for some time after, staring into a snow bank.

A honking city bus startled him, the letter explained, and he motioned for it to pass without him. With the jar secured tightly in both hands, he walked the streets near his dorm until he found another lonely wanderer. The student, also a young man, was thousands of miles from his father and best friend in Mexico City. He carried not a jar but a mesh duffel bag of dirty laundry. John offered to buy the two of them dinner at the nicest restaurant they could find. They sat and talked for hours, comparing childhood mischief and drinking three mugs each of the best hot chocolate either had ever tasted. They became fast friends and together enjoyed a Christmas Eve whose spirit would last a lifetime. The two would pass the tradition along, filling jars of their own and never again looking through the people they encountered each day. John's letter ended: "Thank you for seeing me."

The third letter, addressed to "Our Angel," was from a married woman and high-school dropout. A. J. Francis was born and raised on the south side of the tracks. She and her husband, a childhood sweetheart, had once again fallen behind on their utilities. She suffered through several days of cold weather, with a toddler at home and a husband who worked as a long-haul truck driver. The nearly three hundred dollars in her Christmas jar allowed the gas to be restored immediately. But, more importantly, it instilled in her a new and very strong desire to spend money differently. "I will never see my baby shivering again," the letter said. It went on to describe meeting her husband at the door four days after Christmas with a pen and paper in hand. Together they created a budget so that never again would the lights or the heat or the phone be taken away. "To our angel," she wrote, "you have made my life better. You gave me the one last chance I have been praying for, and I won't let you down."

Hope felt intrigue swirling from her stomach to the hair on the back of her neck. Where had this tradition begun? How widespread was it? How many jars were in circulation? She was familiar with all sorts of holiday goodwill. There were cookies in mailboxes, driveways being shoveled, and volunteers ringing bells outside every grocery store in America so that clothes, food, and medicine could be purchased for the needy.

But Hope knew this Christmas Jar tradition was unique, so unorganized and so seemingly random. There were no sponsors; there was no one to take the much-deserved credit. There was just a collection of nameless, faceless good Samaritans.

She elected—without even a moment of serious inner debate—to spend a day visiting each of the Christmas Jar families. She would present herself both as a representative of the newspaper and as a recipient of a jar herself.

Using resources from the paper and calling in favors she'd accrued over several years of playing back-scratching games, Hope obtained phone numbers and addresses for all three. Her first was a surprise visit to A. J., now living in a warm, middle-class apartment complex with a clean swimming pool and a security gate. The brave woman, who just a few years before was struggling to keep her heat on, was now graduating from cosmetology school. Much to Hope's surprise, A. J. was unwilling to provide many details beyond what Hope already knew from the letter in the paper. She refused to speculate on who might have left the jar and confessed to never having investigated.

When asked about being quoted for Hope's forthcoming article, A. J. responded resolutely, "Darlin', this ain't about gettin' credit. This just don't belong in the papers."

The refrain was similar at the other two stops. Neither had any idea of the jar's origin; none had petitioned beforehand for help from neighbors or churches. All were proud, a little embarrassed, and immeasurably grateful. Each of their lives had improved in ways they could not yet calculate.

In each home, Hope spotted Christmas Jars of their own. One was inconspicuously placed behind a toaster, another high and far back on the refrigerator, and the other partially hidden by a grizzly bear cookie jar. She assumed they were passing the tradition along, but given how little each was willing to share about receiving their own jars, she chose not to waste time pressing for more.

SIX

Stymied and falling behind at the paper, Hope needed to refocus. She relegated the story to spinning deep in her newspaper reporter gears. Two or three times a week she emptied the change from her pockets into an empty dill pickle jar in her kitchen. More than once she considered pitching the experience as a human-interest feature, but knew that without more concrete details it would never fly.

Hope waited. She knew another Christmas would come and, in all probability, so too another round of jars. She would wait for another letter to be printed in the *Daily Record* and pounce. The next time she would investigate deeper, be less forthcoming if that's what it took, and uncover the inspiration and front-page story she knew were hiding just beneath the surface.

On a winter-cool March Saturday morning, Hope learned that a full year of impatience wouldn't be necessary. Another open thank-you letter was printed on page A8.

"Typical me," the letter began. "My wife always handled this sort of thing." Mr. Shane Oaks was a father of five. After she suffered a debilitating nervous breakdown, his wife had moved across the country to live with extended family and seek professional care. He wrote the letter January fourth and addressed the envelope that same afternoon, but then somehow buried it in an inside pocket of his heavy jacket. It had lain there, unremembered for two months.

The detailed letter chronicled perhaps his most meaningful Christmas Eve ever. The forty-three-year-old man awoke early and ventured into the biting cold to retrieve the morning paper yet again from the bushes along the front of his house. "But I don't blame him for his terrible aim," he wrote of the young carrier who delivered papers each morning before school. "He's a real hard worker. I admire that.

"I opened the door," the letter wove on, "fetched the paper, and when I turned to step back inside my home, noticed a jar full of money sitting on the floor by my crashed-on-the-couch son." The letter continued and explained that after breakfast, Shane and his children counted over five hundred dollars in cash and change. The money allowed him to sneak out later on Christmas Eve to the only store still open and buy a few small gifts for his children. The unexpectedly enormous costs of daycare had decimated his plans for much of a holiday.

"I need you to know that I did not spend it all," he wrote, "just enough to add color to my children's Christmas morning." The letter stated that the balance of the money would go toward beginner books for the youngest, groceries, and badly needed school supplies.

"Thank you, whoever you are, for the generous jar and the lesson it taught us. The money did not save my life," the letter ended, "but it did save my faith in men."

Hope took her feet and jogged across the room, grabbed a phone book under the receptionist's desk, and blazed across the parking lot to her car. Within forty-five minutes she was knocking on Mr. Oaks's front door.

He welcomed her in, and in rapid-fire fashion she shared her own experience and the few details she'd gleaned from the other families. "What do you think the common thread is?" she asked. "Do you think it's someone you know? Or is it someone who from a distance saw your plight and felt pity and gave what they could?"

"I have no idea," he answered, apparently to all her questions at once. "But I'm so grateful, so *very* grateful," he repeated, and though he wanted to respect the giver's anonymity, he admitted to having a hunch.

"My oldest is a night owl." The man's cadence suggested experience weaving good bedtime stories. "Sometimes he comes downstairs with all the lights off and just sits. He says he meditates, but I think he talks to his mother. Either way, I allow it. Just as long as he's not a zombie at school and keeps his head together. He's my right arm, you know."

"Sounds like a sweet kid." Hope knew all about talking to a faraway mother. She'd been doing it for months.

"So Noah, my son, is sitting quietly in my chair when he hears footsteps outside. He got on all fours and crawled to the window and saw two figures tiptoeing on the porch and leaving something on the step at the door."

"What time was that?" Hope's reporter juices were at full flow.

"Late. Probably two o'clock, somewhere around there."

"Interesting." Hope scribbled indecipherable notes on her pad.

"They left the jar wrapped in a towel and hustled back to the sidewalk and around the corner. Noah brought the jar inside, set it on the floor next to him, and eventually fell asleep where he lay."

"Do you have the towel? May I see it?"

"Why not?" He left the room and returned a few seconds later. The hand towel featured twelve drummers, using red-and-white candy canes as drumsticks. "It's really nice," Hope offered. "Handmade, I bet."

"If you say so."

"OK, this is good. This is *very* good." Hope felt like a cub reporter on the verge of breaking the story of the year. "So who do you think it was? Who does your son think it was? Any ideas?"

"To be honest, I don't think they want us playing Sherlock Holmes with this. I'm sure they didn't expect my seventeen-year-old to be watching through a slit in the drapes."

"Understood." She needed to assure him that she would handle his disclosures with care. "But this is such an amazing story, such a meaningful thing these folks are doing. If the paper agrees to run my story, think of the good it could do."

"I don't know." He wriggled. "I've probably said too much already."

Her response was comfortably rehearsed. "Sir, my paper spends half its ink, probably more, reporting the countless ills of the world, reporting on every page stories of human weakness. As someone in the business I get pretty worn out by it all. Don't you?"

"I've lived it. Lived my share. I know . . ."

"I am sorry, I *am*, I just think there is so little . . . so little positive news out there, that we should expose . . . no, I mean *showcase* the good whenever we can. We can remind people that there is plenty of charity in the world, and in our city."

Maybe Mom was right, she thought. *I could be a politician with that knack for spin.*

She let the sermon hang for a moment. "Sir?"

"Of course we don't know for certain, but Noah's pretty sure they live a few streets over. They're twin girls, and I expect he thinks they're worth looking at, if you know what I mean."

"Oh, I see." Hope pursed her lips playfully.

"Their parents run a furniture repair business or something in their garage. We've seen the girls come and go from there quite a lot."

"Thank you!" She was ready again with her spiraled notepad. "So you know their names?"

"No. But my wife probably did." His voice trailed off.

"This is rough for you. The holiday must be difficult—"

"It's fine," he interrupted. "We're all right. But thank you."

She imagined his letter in the paper would generate more than his share of pity.

"I can tell you what house it is, but remember, we're just guessing here." He drew her a map on a pink piece of paper from a strawberry-scented notepad. "And you didn't hear this from me, got it?"

"Of course." Hope's story of the Christmas Jar— her front-page feature—was practically writing itself.

———.———

Hope sat for ninety minutes in a neighborhood pancake house, reevaluating and retooling her approach. With one hand she scribbled notes on a pad. With the other she dipped French fries into a sauce she'd concocted of two parts ketchup, two parts mayonnaise, and a small squirt of mustard. All three previous visits to Christmas Jar families had yielded so little information, until this evening. *This will be the story that makes me.*

The decision to play loose with the truth was made so quickly, and with so little reflection, that it surprised even Hope. She coated her last fry in the pinkish sauce and dropped it in her mouth.

This isn't just about a story, she justified, *it's about saying thank you to a legion of angels.*

SEVEN

Hope rolled up to 316 Oakliegh Hill, stopped the car, and breathed deeply for thirty seconds, just the way her mother had taught. She surveyed the property and noticed the converted two-car garage. A wide single rolling door was shut, and the words "Restored, Inc." were painted in tall white letters on a golden oval background above the door. She stepped out of her car and walked with purpose down the sidewalk and up the stairs to the spacious porch. Individually carved capital block letters were screwed into the brick above the polished handworked wooden front door: "MAXWELL."

Hope knocked.

After an unusually long wait, an attractive woman—probably in her mid-forties, Hope judged—appeared with an inviting smile.

"Good evening, ma'am. My name is Hope Jensen. I'm a college student, a senior actually, and I wonder if I could ask a few questions about your furniture business for a project I'm doing." The words flowed easily, like a seasoned sales pitch.

"I suppose so." The woman's voice was as pleasant as her soft, youthful face.

"Thank you." Hope stepped through the door. *I'm in.*

The woman left her standing in the foyer and vanished around the corner. She returned, again after an uncomfortably long wait, with a man Hope assumed was her husband. He was salt-and-pepper gray, but mostly salt. His chin and nose were large and distinguished but not distracting. His eyes were wood-paneling brown.

"Hello." Hope stuck her hand out.

"Hi there," he answered, firmly taking her hand but just holding it more than shaking it.

He and his wife led Hope into the adjoining living room, where he sat down on a worn brown cloth recliner. "My wife says you're curious about our furniture operation here." He worked his back and lower body side to side into the crease of the chair until he looked comfortable.

"Operation?" Hope asked.

"Our business, our family business."

"Of course." Hope's palms were already sweating. "Yes, I am. But have I caught you at a bad time?"

"Certainly not," he answered. "Have a seat." He motioned to a love seat across the room.

"I was telling your wife—"

"It's Lauren," the man's wife said.

"But you can call her gorgeous; I do," he added instantly, as if part of a polished routine. "And I'm Adam."

Lauren breathed a melodramatic what-am-I-going-to-do-with-him sigh. She sat in a chair at her husband's side. Hope sensed the chair knew her well.

"It's great to meet you both. I'm Hope. And thanks again for allowing me a few minutes."

"So what kind of college class has a doll like yourself out after dark?" Hope had met only a few people in her life she thought could pull off the risky trick of calling a strange woman "doll." Adam was one of them.

"I'm on schedule to graduate this spring, fingers crossed, but to get through my senior advanced writing class I need to profile a small or home-based business." Even as the words left her lips she wondered if her departed mother would approve of the white lie. It was one of the rare occasions Hope prayed Louise was not watching from an invisible perch nearby.

"We certainly qualify as both," Adam said. "What kinds of things you looking for?"

"As you know, sir, your type of business is the heart of America. It's small businesses that make our economy go. And I'm looking to find out why. What makes them successful? What challenges do they face that, say, Fortune 500s don't?"

At some point during her lengthy answer, Adam playfully put his right hand over his heart. "Amen!" The deep wrinkles around his mouth gave away a healthy sense of humor.

"Be good, Adam, for goodness' sake." Hope imagined his wife used that phrase rather often. "We'd be happy to help," she added. "Sounds like a noble assignment."

"Thank you, ma'am." Hope tried to hide an enormous exhale.

A loud noise yanked their eyes from each other and toward a ringing coming from somewhere on the other side of the house.

"Excuse me." Lauren rose to answer the phone. As she kissed her husband on the forehead, Hope envisioned for the first time the headline being printed on the massive steel printer in the warehouse that adjoined the *Daily Record* offices. The papers are folded and stacked on a chain conveyor belt. Her co-workers gather with her at the end of the line, and she lifts from the belt the first fully assembled paper of the day. Her article is running above the fold on A1.

"Tomorrow." His voice scratched the silence. Hope could tell he wasn't used to whispering.

"Sir?"

"Come back tomorrow, around lunchtime. Not

much I can really show you tonight. Come tomorrow, and I'll give the grand tour, show you where the magic happens for Restored. We'll talk shop." He was chortling before the pun was all the way out of his mouth.

"Tomorrow, then. Thank you, sir." She took her feet. "I can show myself out." Hope reached down for another full handshake, and Adam held on for an extra second, smiling into her. *This man has stories to tell,* she thought, smiling back.

She walked to the door, hearing in the distance his wife end her phone call with a loving good-bye. Hope wished she could hide under the rug to hear their discussion after the door shut.

She stayed up late, writing a legal-size sheet of questions to ask the family she suspected might be at the center of the Christmas Jar tradition. Something in her said the story of Adam and Lauren Maxwell was bigger than a few random acts of kindness. This had either become something tremendous, and the Maxwells knew why, or it was *about* to, and they were the *reason* why. For now, Hope's strategy was to keep her research—and her story—to herself and away from the *Daily Record.* But her reporter's intuition insisted that a remarkable story was on the verge of appearing on the front page.

EIGHT

Hope returned as promised the next afternoon. She bypassed the front door and walked toward the converted garage. The door was open, and the sound of an electric sander buzzed. "Welcome back," Adam Maxwell yelled and gestured through a cloud of peach sawdust. He plucked the power cord from a suspended plug and pulled caked plastic goggles from his eyes.

"We meet again," Hope began.

"Indeed. Welcome to our humble *operation*," Adam teased, and squeezed her arm, reaching by her for a wet rag slung over the back of a tall wooden stool. "Sit."

Hope surveyed the workshop while he wiped sawdust from between his fingers. "So this is it? This is where you make all your furniture?" Journalism had taught her to lead with the most obvious questions, slowly engendering trust.

"Not *my* furniture," he answered firmly. "*Your* furniture. We restore and refinish used furniture; we don't actually make any."

"I see, so you—"

"Actually, I guess we do make a few pieces here and again," he continued as if not hearing her. "Like that stool you're on. Made that."

"Really?"

"And that." He nodded at a credenza against the back wall.

"Fascinating."

"Fascinating? You're an easy sell."

"No, really. I think it's neat to run your own show, from right here in your house."

"It has its advantages," he replied just as Lauren entered from their home through a side door. "Like that," he said, tossing the rag toward his wife. "Hey, gorgeous."

"You need help with him, sweetheart, you just call,"

Lauren said to Hope. "Don't let him wear you out with stories."

"Exactly why I'm here, ma'am."

"It's Lauren, but thank your mother for your manners, would you?"

"I will." Hope doubted they would ever know her well enough to learn her mother was gone.

"I'm off to the store. Easy day today, right, Adam?" Lauren gave him a faux dirty look. It was obviously not the first time.

"Yes, L, easy day, lots of breaks, no loud music, no junk food."

Lauren rolled her eyes. "Good luck with him, Hope." She shook her head. "I'll undo any damage to you later if need be." She turned and stepped back through the door, shutting it behind her.

"I thought she'd never leave." Adam wiped his forehead. Ten minutes there and already Hope saw a kind of love she'd never seen up close. "So what do you need to know to guarantee yourself an A on this thing you're writing?"

"I guess everything. Tell me about your family,

how this all started, what it takes to make this sort of thing work. I've read lots of horror stories about family businesses."

"They're all true." He laughed.

"'Here? I don't believe it. It seems so perfect."

"You know what they say about the weather 'round here? Same holds true in my workshop. Just stand by for five minutes, it'll change."

"That's fair. I'll withhold judgment."

"Deal." Adam rested his hands on his hips. "So this is it. This is our life here." His long arms reached out and swept the room. "We restore furniture; we make things beautiful again. Been doing it since I was in college, before Lauren and I met. It's all we know."

Adam continued talking—sometimes, it seemed, to himself—and they began their first hour together. He walked her around the crowded shop floor, introducing her to tools, stains, clamps, and more brushes than she'd ever seen in one drawer. Hope found herself more interested than she'd expected to be.

"That's pretty neat, working with your wife all these years."

"It's a blessing that I wouldn't trade for anything . . ." His voice trailed off. Though his voice had the distinct quaver that suggested the presence of tears, Hope saw none.

"You all right, sir?"

"The legacy," he continued, ignoring—or not hearing—the question, "the legacy of a family business is that every product you sell or service you provide is a piece of you. Our family, the girls included, put our souls into each piece we restore. For the three or four weeks most pieces are in our care, they become ours. It's a deep trust people put in you. Daycare for furniture, I call it."

He's an open book, Hope thought, *of very cheesy lines.* She liked him already.

"You hear that?" Adam asked, cupping his ear.

"I . . . I don't know. What?"

"The lunch whistle. Sandwich time." Adam walked to the door. "Let's eat."

"No, sir, I couldn't."

"Couldn't eat? Sure you could. Come."

Hope followed him into the kitchen and adjoining nook.

"What can I make ya?"

"Anything's fine. Two of whatever you're making yourself." Hope watched him pull a Tupperware container of sandwich fixings from a crisper drawer and set up a mini assembly line on the longest counter. Her eyes scanned the room and stopped on the real reason she was about to share lunch with the kind Mr. Adam Maxwell. Sitting partially hidden behind an upright joke-a-day calendar was a glass jar filled with change and a surprising number of bills. Written across its front, presumably in permanent marker, were the letters "CJ."

Bingo, she almost said aloud.

He put finishing touches on their ham-and-swiss hoagies, poured two glasses of grape juice, and said a quick blessing. "A Maxwell special. You're quite a lucky lady."

"I am," Hope answered honestly. "Yes, I am."

After lunch she picked up her plate and glass and followed him into the kitchen. "What's this?" Hope asked, taking her chance and reaching for the jar. "Petty cash?"

"Not exactly," Adam answered, taking the jar from her. "It's just a jar."

"A jar full of spare change. I like it. Like an old-school savings account."

"You could say that." Adam returned the jar to its spot, rotating it until the "CJ" was hidden from view.

"Sounds like there's a story hidden in the bottom of that thing," Hope fished.

"Doll, there are stories hidden in every jar." Adam ran warm water over the plates, though it didn't appear they needed it, and then loaded them into the dishwasher. "Ready to work?"

"Ready when you are." The seed of curiosity was planted. Hope would wait.

The two returned to the garage, and Hope paced him with questions about the business. "When did you start?" "How do you market?" "What other jobs have you had?" For two hours Adam played along and proudly displayed several projects-in-progress. His answers to Hope's phony questions grew increasingly more interesting.

Hope stopped checking her watch, and eventually Lauren returned home and put a polite end to their interview. "Come back any time you like," she said. "If you need more, I assure you this man will gladly tell all."

"I'd love to come back." Hope hid her elation. "We didn't get much into the business side of things."

"Anytime," Adam offered. "We sure *hope* you get an A."

Hope smiled big. "Been waiting for that all afternoon, haven't you, sir?"

"Maybe . . ."

They said good-bye and scheduled another visit in three days. Hope drove back to the newspaper, jotting notes at stop signs and whistling "Jingle Bells."

The two-hour chats were repeated every three or four days for a month. On her third visit, Hope met and befriended the twin daughters, Clara and Julie, and their omnipresent boyfriends. The twins were alumni at the same local college from which Hope had graduated, though they operated under the impression Hope was still in school. No matter; Hope played the part of ragged college student like a pro.

On her next visit, Hope was introduced to Hannah, the eldest of the three Maxwell children. She was thirty-two and newly married, and she and her husband, Dustin, had their sights set on taking over Restored when Adam and Lauren were ready to cruise around the country in their rebuilt convertible Mustang.

Hope often expressed awe at the children's ability to manage marriages and social lives, keep an eye on their parents, and still take a role in the family business. *All this,* she thought, *from a family of five running a highly successful and locally respected business from a dusty garage. This would make a great college report.*

Adam's love of storytelling helped Hope assemble an impressive dossier on the family. More than once, Hope drove home imagining her front-page story becoming a four- or five-part series, and then a best-selling book. But oddly, Hope became so ensconced in her fascination with the Maxwells that she

almost forgot what originally sent her to their door—
that is, until an unexpected Sunday brunch.

Adam and Hope were sitting at a table in the corner of the garage looking at advertisements the family
had run in a regional crafter's magazine.

"All right, you two." Lauren's head appeared
around the doorway. "Brunch is on. The kids are here."

"Oh, no, you really don't need to feed me again."

"Of course we don't *need* to, Hope. We *want* to."

"I—"

"You'd love to? Outstanding. Bring Mr. Sawdust
with you."

They washed their hands and sat around a beau-
tifully crafted dining room table. Hope could not
remember her last meal with real linens and silverware. Adam offered a short blessing, thanking God
for the meal before them, thanking Him for the hands
that made it, and thanking Him for the gift of Hope
at their table. She could tell he smiled when he said
"Hope."

"Thank you, sir," she said humbly when he finished.

They ate crepes with fresh fruit, hash browns, and hot rolls. "These might be the best rolls I've ever tasted," Hope said.

"Thank you, dear. But the recipe belonged to Adam's mother; she gets the credit. It wasn't easy, but I wrestled it from her. Believe it or not, I actually had to *practice* with her. It took years of Thanksgiving dinner rehearsals before she entrusted me with it." Lauren finished the story, which led to another by her talented storytelling husband, and one more by each of the children. Hope saw the perfect opportunity to fish.

"Speaking of stories," she began, and the chatter around the table came to an abrupt end. "May I ask about the jar? What is the big, secret story of the change jar in the kitchen?"

For a family of so many words, the inquiry was met with surprising silence.

"Curious are we?" Adam twirled his fork and stabbed the largest strawberry left. "We could tell you, but then we'd have to—"

"It's a family thing," Lauren interrupted.

"I apologize. I didn't know." Hope wiped her

mouth with her cloth napkin, even though there was nothing there, and replaced the napkin on her lap. She looked down and readjusted it, waiting to be rescued.

"Come on, Dad," Hannah implored.

"Yeah, Dad, tell it, tell it." The twins chanted like playful young children.

"You think she's ready?" Adam sat back in his chair and grabbed the table on either side of his plate.

"That's up to you, sweetheart," said Lauren.

"Ready for what?" Hope could hardly contain herself.

"To the family room!" Adam shouted, and pointed across the table and into the next room.

"Here we go," Hannah said to her husband, taking him by the hand and leading him to the love seat. Lauren and Hope cleared the table, and Adam staked out his chair next to the fireplace.

"Enjoy this. It's special," Lauren said to Hope as they stacked plates next to the sink for washing. "And rare . . ."

Hope feared her heart was beating loud enough for

the neighbors to hear. They left the dishes for later and joined the rest.

Adam Maxwell, master craftsman of both words and wood, began to weave a story that would forever change the way Hope viewed her place in the world.

NINE

"Honey, don't forget the Crisco for my hips." Frank Maxwell made the same joke every year. "We'll need it to get me out from this chair." As he'd done twenty-six times before, he called out to his wife, Dora, as she walked into the kitchen with an armful of dirty dishes.

"Yes, dear, the Crisco. Coming right up." The response—and courtesy chuckle—were always the same.

For the Maxwell family, Thanksgiving dinner was an annual eating contest. They ate their own weight in turkey, mashed potatoes with skins, Waldorf salad, and hot homemade rolls with real butter. There was never concern about weeks of lingering leftovers. After dessert they gathered in the TV room for pro football and Christmas planning—who was going where, who wanted what, and who was tasked with visiting the lovable and loony Cousin Gregg, forever a guest at the Greenbrier Adult Developmental Center.

Adam and Lauren, the newlyweds, spoke first. "If it's all right, Mom," Adam said, "we would really like to do our thing this year. It's our first Christmas, and we'd like to sorta be alone."

"And miss my Christmas dinner?" his mother said, delivering a mild dose of guilt.

"No, Mother, just Christmas Eve and morning. We'll come by later." As the oldest of four, Adam felt a sense of responsibility for his mom and dad that his younger siblings did not entirely grasp. Avoiding them altogether was never an option.

One by one the others laid out their plans. Steven, the second oldest, would be out of town, visiting in-laws in Pittsburgh.

"Taking my grandbaby with you?"

"Yes, Grandma, we're taking the baby," answered Steven's sweet wife, Lisa. "But don't worry, you'll still get your sloppy Christmas kiss on the way out of town." Lisa loved her mother-in-law like her own mother— almost.

Terri, the only daughter, was alone this year. Her husband, Marshall Young, an army chaplain, was stationed overseas and not set to return for another eight months. She worked double shifts as a nurse at a Veterans Administration hospital two towns away, and since Terri would have no reason to be home, her mother expected to see a lot of her during the holidays. "*I'll* be here, Mother," she said, grinning with sarcasm, as if she were the only one who cared.

"Thanks, Sis," Adam offered. "You were *always* Mom's favorite."

Terri threw a green velvet pillow from the love seat across the room, hitting Adam squarely in the head. He collapsed on the floor, rolling over in feigned agony.

"All right, you two," Dora stepped in. Frank was still engrossed in football. "How about you, JJ?" She turned to Jeff, the youngest Maxwell, who had gone by JJ since another boy also named Jeff moved in four years earlier with a reputation for setting fires on peoples' doorsteps.

"Oh, boy, ladies and gents, do I have one rocking Christmas planned!" The spunky seventeen-year-old swung his legs around the piano bench he had been straddling and launched into a popping, improvisational version of "Jingle-Bell Rock." JJ was always onstage, even in his living room.

> *Jingle-bell, Jingle-bell, Jingle-bell Rock,*
> *I've got a concert Christmas Eve.*
> *The senior jazz band is playing a show,*
> *And I'll wear long sleeves!*
> *The gals will swooooon and the jocks will turn green,*
> *As we have a ball.*
> *The Broadway bigwigs will clap along,*
> *As we rock the mall!*

He laughed at his clever tune and played on, thinking of a second verse as his older brothers and sister tried not to encourage him with laughter of their own. It was no use.

"Now, don't encourage the boy," Dad said from

his recliner, his eyes fixed on the halftime show but his ears enjoying the sounds of an entire family back under the same roof, if even for only a few hours. "You're a nutty bunch," he yelled out. "Nuttier than a squirrel's pantry." He was a living, breathing book of bad jokes.

The evening wore on comfortably, like favorite socks, and the pride and joy of Frank and Dora Maxwell said good night to their parents and set off on their independent ways. Another Thanksgiving had passed without incident. Good health, good humor, and good tradition were safely on their side.

"I just love your mom," Lauren said, kicking her shoes off, reclining back, and putting her feet on the dashboard.

"That'll pass," Adam deadpanned.

"She's sweet, really genuine, you know?"

"Genuinely batty? I concur."

"Genuinely your *mother*. Your *mother*, Adam."

"I'm kidding. It's Thanksgiving humor. She's a real doll."

"I have never, ever seen a family tease like yours does. Has it always been like that?"

"Only since I was born, and I'm the oldest." Adam let the joke set in. "Come on, L, it's healthy."

"Whatever you say"—she smiled before even finishing—"Mr. Receding Hairline."

"Hey!"

"It's healthy, *healthy!*"

"Shoulda seen that coming." Adam changed the subject. "So, shopping tomorrow? It's the first day of the season."

"I don't know. The girls invited me, but it's sure no fun without money."

"So spend a little," he answered. "Why not?"

"Right, spend money we don't have; now *that* makes sense."

Adam and Lauren were the definition of frugal. A year before meeting Lauren and three full years before marrying her, Adam had opened a furniture restoration business. He called it Restored, Inc., and so far it provided a steady, though modest, income. Lauren managed the books and marketing; Adam did the restoring.

He converted their single-car garage into a functional studio. It was filled with saws, sanders, hand tools, wood stains, brushes and brooms, and on some days the unmistakable smell of freshly cut, untreated wood. For Adam, the aroma was almost intoxicating.

Lauren gathered and pulled her black hair over her right shoulder and into view. She rubbed her fingers around a dozen hairs, monitoring a few split ends. "How about something different?" She pulled a single hair from her head and began twirling it around her index finger. "How about we save a little and put a can, like a soup can or even an empty jar, on the counter. We put our change in it every night. Pocket change."

"And?" Adam was curious.

"And we buy presents for one another with the money, whatever we save but not a penny more. It's a limited budget. How much can we possibly save in a few weeks? Call it forced self-restraint." She sounded like a financial planner.

"Okay. I'll bite. Let's do it." They shook on it, as

if closing a business deal, and pulled into their driveway. As always, they had talked themselves all the way home.

In the morning, Lauren washed out a near-empty jar of blackberry jelly and placed it on the counter by the phone. On it she painted "The Christmas Jar" in green and red model paint. On the bottom she added three letters: "ALM." Adam and Lauren Maxwell.

The days and weeks rolled on, and Christmas arrived, as always, before they were ready. They stopped work early on December twenty-fourth and emptied the jar on the kitchen table that Adam had made in high school.

"Twenty-seven dollars and eighty-eight cents," Lauren announced. "Not bad, huh?" She sounded as sheepish as she felt. "Sorry, Adam. I thought we'd find a little more."

"That's crazy talk, L. It's plenty. In fact, it's *perfect.*" He rose from his chair and kissed her on top of the head. "You start rolling them and I'll sneak to the couch for a nap. Wake me when you're done." He paused in the doorway, waiting for something to hit him from behind. It never came. He cautiously looked back, his eyes half-closed, and found her spinning a quarter on the table and mumbling to herself.

"L?" Adam returned to his seat. "What's wrong?"

"Thirteen dollars and ninety-four cents. Each. That's it. That's not quite what I had in mind. That's not much of a Christmas."

"Sweetheart, it's plenty. It's Christmas. Everything I ever wanted, everything I ever asked for, everything I've ever needed is sitting right here. Look, you wake up tomorrow morning healthy, smiling, and still speaking to me, and I'll have the best Christmas ever."

"You're a good man," she answered with a frog in her throat.

Adam reached across the table and scooped his half of the Christmas budget into the tail of his untucked shirt. "Let's go shopping."

They drove to the nearest mega department store, parked in the farthest space, put on sunglasses they didn't need, and synchronized their watches. Hand in hand, they weaved through the cars and in through the automatic doors. They split up, pockets bulging with change, off on a mission to buy their first-ever Christmas presents as a married couple. The plan was to buy them together, in the same cavernous store, but keep them hidden all the way home.

Like cartoon spies, they bobbed and weaved around the store, in search of thirteen dollars' worth of Christmas joy. At one point Adam hid under a rack of wool winter coats when Lauren got too close for comfort. Another time, just before their scheduled meet-up at the front doors, Lauren turned herself into a mannequin in the men's sportswear department. Adam walked past, pretending not to see her and whistling the theme to *Mission Impossible* as he strolled by.

At registers as far apart as physically possible, they counted out their Christmas Jar change, much to the chagrin of those behind them. With their gifts triple-bagged for privacy, they sped home and disappeared to opposite ends of the house to wrap. And Christmas Eve became Christmas morning.

They slept until 9:00. By 9:10, Adam was mixing chocolate pancake batter in the kitchen.

"Good morning, Mrs. Claus." He pulled her chair

out as she wiped sleep from her tired eyes. "What do you think, breakfast first? Or presents?"

"*Adam.*" She seemed to disapprove. "A good breakfast is the most important part of the day."

He nodded his head and pivoted on his heels back to the kitchen counter.

"But not *today! Presents!*" She pushed away from the table and raced into the family room.

"Stop, you sneak!" Adam called and chased her, tackling her from behind and sending them both into the base of the four-foot-tall Christmas tree. Adam caught it from falling with his right arm and pushed it back up, resetting it firmly into its plastic water base. "Just for that"—he was playfully stern—"I get to be Santa."

Lauren knew the routine; she had experienced a Maxwell Christmas two years before in the role of the visiting girlfriend and last year as the fiancée. Santa got to pull the presents from the tree, read the tag, and deliver them one at a time to the appointed spots. Lauren's spot was on the couch.

There were the gifts they had bought one another,

a few from both sets of parents, and several from the siblings.

"Me first," Lauren said, pulling the tape off her first gift with great care. It was a pink tube of bubble-gum lip gloss. She applied a thick coat and gave him a sloppy kiss on the cheek, leaving his dimple a greasy crater. "Perfect," she declared.

He opened his first gift, a pair of tomato-red reindeer socks with eyes, nose, and tiny foam antlers. "Yes!" he yelled and tossed the socks in the air. "I wanted these! I saw them on the 'On Sale' rack up front and crossed my fingers that one day we could meet again. Thanks, L."

Lauren's next gift was a wooden, Western-themed picture frame. "Who's the cutie on the horse, huh?" Lauren jabbed, referring to the blue-eyed, blonde model twirling a lasso and sporting a cheesy grin.

"Just a girl I dated in college."

She whacked him with his own new sock before the sentence could settle. "You dated *me* in college," she said with emphasis.

"Oh, whoops."

Adam then opened a jumbo pack of razors, something he actually needed. He'd been shaving with an old one for two weeks too long. The excitement continued through the other assorted gifts, though never as rich as the moments they shared opening the ones from each other. "Great idea, L. *Great* idea." They shared a long hug, and Adam returned to his pancake project.

Later that afternoon they worked side by side on an armoire they had promised to have finished for a client by January first. They hand-sanded in rhythm and sang along to a paint-flecked portable stereo blaring the Beach Boys.

For dinner they visited Adam's parents. They feasted on ham, dressing, cheesy potatoes, and, of course, hot rolls. They hugged everyone twice and drove home. Lauren kicked off her shoes and wedged her feet up in between the windshield and the dashboard. She was wearing Adam's reindeer socks.

The season passed in harmony, and that was all they'd ever known to ask for. Spring was short, but summer dragged on longer than normal. As the dog days of August wore on, Lauren caught herself thinking of Christmas as she visited the grand opening of a new downtown boutique. She called her husband.

"Hi, sweetie, what ya doin'?"

"Working, dear. Getting set to finish the Myers's dresser."

"Great! Right on schedule."

"What do you need, L? My hands are full."

"Nothing important. Just thinking about Christmas."

"You know we've not even seen September first yet, right?"

"I know," she assured him. "But think about it. Once you hit Labor Day, the rest is just around the corner."

Adam sighed and waited for whatever was up her sleeve.

"I thought we might try the jar again this year, but earlier, you know, to save more money."

"Sure, that sounds smart. Let's talk about it

tonight." Adam looked at his watch and felt the pressure of an afternoon melting into evening.

"How about we start Labor Day weekend? Just pocket change. Just like last year."

"Labor Day it is. Now, get home soon. The studio misses you." They hung up, and Adam, shaking his head, said aloud, "That girl's nuttier than Dumbo's pantry."

The Christmas Jar appeared back on the counter sometime in the early evening after a holiday barbeque of chicken and corn on the cob. As the holidays crept closer, and without ever conspiring to do so, Adam and Lauren began shopping with bills to generate more spare change.

The morning of Christmas Eve they counted the change at the kitchen table before breakfast.

"Sixty-two dollars, twenty-one cents," Adam said, surprised by the total. "And lots more dimes this year than last." They divided the money. "Thirty-one ten, and *you* get the extra penny, big spender." He slid her share across the table. "We'll go after lunch?"

"After lunch," answered Lauren, but both would

spend every second before then thinking how best to stretch their fortunes.

With too many coins to manage, and a desire not to make another round of cash register enemies, they stopped by the bank and had their Christmas Jar haul converted into bills. They drove to the shopping center, set a time limit, and split up. Forty-five minutes later they met at the car, gifts tucked under their coats. Arriving home, they wasted no time hiding at opposite ends of the house to do their wrapping.

Christmas morning was familiar. They awoke, earlier than the year before, and skipped breakfast. Lauren crawled behind the six-foot-tall tree; it was her turn to be Santa.

"Heeeads up!" Her voice rose high as she tossed a gift to his designated spot. In just a minute or two the gifts were evenly divided. They started with the in-law gifts, saving each other's for last.

When they got to the gifts from each other, Lauren unwrapped a much nicer picture frame than the year before, this time with their own wedding photo inside, and an ounce of perfume he'd seen her test on her wrists weeks before.

Adam opened a package of designer dress socks and a popular but inexpensive electric rotary razor. "Perfect," he said, inserting the accompanying batteries. He rubbed it quickly over his chin and grabbed her hand. "Smooooooooth!" The word dragged on for five seconds. "I'll be more irresistible than ever."

Lauren batted her eyelids and lifted her picture frame. She and her handsome young groom stood beaming before a water fountain shooting high in the air and in a dozen different directions. "What did I get myself into?" she asked the eight-by-ten. "I've married a maniac."

After opening their gifts, they ate a cold-cereal brunch. It was another memorable Christmas. "Of all of them," Adam teased, "this was absolutely, positively the very bestest."

On June first of the following year they decided over deep-dish pizza to work on having a child. They had been married eighteen months and saw no reason to wait. Adam raised his frosted root beer. "To our first—a beautiful, left-handed baby boy with a ninety-five-mile-an-hour fastball."

"To a healthy baby with ten fingers and ten toes," she countered, knocking her mug into his.

"Cheers!"

Adam suggested they start their next Christmas Jar in July. "That gives us a few more months to save, buy some nice things for the baby, right?" She readily agreed. On July Fourth the jar was set in its usual place.

A creative marketing plan with the local phone book boosted business that summer, and by the time the leaves fell, Restored was busier than ever. By Thanksgiving, the jar was nearly full. By Christmas Eve, coins were gingerly placed on top, rising slightly above the opening. Careful placement was all that kept several dollars' worth of change from spilling onto the Formica counter.

They counted before breakfast and were thrilled with just over one hundred dollars. "That's a lot of spare change, L," Adam said, piling the coins in high stacks around the table. Once again they visited the bank before heading to their now traditional department store. They agreed that with more money they would need more time. They settled on one hour and used every minute.

Now in its third year, Christmas morning at the Maxwells' home was becoming an institution. The tree—no longer an inexpensive artificial model—brushed the ceiling at eight glorious feet. Smells were sweeter, gifts ever more thoughtful, and memories carefully logged away into their most treasured places.

TEN

That's quite a unique tradition." Hope broke Adam's rhythm, and suddenly all were transported from Adam's entertaining tale back to their comfortable spots in the Maxwell living room. Hope baited him for more. "So every year you fill the jar and use the money to buy presents for one another? Your pocket change basically pays for Christmas?"

"You're half right," Adam responded. "But Hannah over there put a kink in our plans. Didn't you, darling?"

She promptly buried her reddening face into her husband's chest. "You can stop now, Dad."

"Oh, Hannah Banana, let him go," her mother piped in. "Your father's on a roll."

Lauren was finally pregnant and showing, and the anticipation of the arrival of Adam and Lauren's first child was exhilarating. With another set of hands to open presents that year, they started their now-annual Christmas Jar on Easter weekend. Winter approached, and both became adept at accumulating change. Whenever possible, they asked for coins rather than small bills at convenience and drug stores, the post office, and so on. Between Thanksgiving and Christmas they were blessed with a stunningly perfect baby girl. They named her Hannah.

Once again on Christmas Eve, Adam and Lauren emptied their jar on the kitchen table. "A new record," Adam announced. "Two hundred fifty-five dollars and seventy cents." They converted it to bills and trekked off for the ritual spree. That year they bought a few nice things for one another, but it was the baby that scored the biggest haul. They opened their packages and enjoyed a quiet Christmas afternoon as a family of three. That night, after dinner at Adam's parents', they decided that now with a child and a desire to create a lasting tradition, they would begin leaving the jar on the counter and fill it year round. They started December twenty-sixth, and their first full year yielded over four hundred dollars.

Over the following years, the tradition became family law. Then after a miscarriage at eleven weeks, Lauren and Adam were surprised with not one but *two* identically perfect baby girls. Now with ample experience at hoarding change, and even more Maxwells to please on Christmas morning, they saw their once modest-sized jar grow from a jelly jar to a Mason jar to a giant dill-pickle jar that rose almost eighteen inches high.

During the next two years they asked earlier than ever for their change to be made in coins. By then, even the two-year-old twins knew to remind their mother. "Get silver, Mommy, silver!" They knew the game. No matter what, all coins went into the jar at the end of every single day. And in the Maxwell tradition, there were no exceptions. Or so they thought.

During their tenth year of marriage and after ten Maxwell Christmas Jars, the family of five set off to the bank on Christmas Eve afternoon with their most impressive collection of spare change ever. It was Hannah's turn to bask in the privilege of carrying the jar, and the seven-year-old struggled to carry the jar from the family van.

While Adam and Lauren wrestled the sleepy twins from their car seats and into a double-wide stroller, Hannah's eyes spotted a heavy woman in a gray sweat suit sitting on the curb, crying into one hand and holding a thin slip of white paper in the other.

Adam and Lauren made their way into the bank and settled in the teller line, still consoling the grouchy twins and unaware of Hannah's whereabouts. Outside the heavily tinted windows, Hannah approached the disheveled woman.

"What's wrong?" Hannah asked bravely. "Are you sad?" To her parents' consternation, she'd never been afraid of strangers. "Hello?" She sat down and placed the jar between them.

The woman sat motionless, her hands on her stomach.

"Hello?" Hannah repeated. She was too young to

read the signs; any adult would have given up after the first hello.

"Ma'am, would you like our Christmas Jar?"

The question opened the woman's eyes, and the shadow of a smile appeared.

"Please. Please take our Christmas Jar." With both hands the dogged little girl slid the jar a few inches until it rested against the woman's left leg.

Adam, at last aware that Hannah had never followed her family into the lobby, raced outside. "Hannah!" he yelled, spotting her engaged with the stranger on the curb. "Hannah, are you all right?"

Meanwhile Lauren stood watching through the thick windows. One hand rocked the twins' stroller back and forth, and the other rested on the cool glass. Peace filled her, and though it had been playing since October everywhere she went, she heard Christmas music for the first time playing in the background.

Adam crouched at his daughter's side. "What's up, Hannah?"

The woman suddenly spoke. "Nothing, sir, it's nothing. Your sweet daughter offered me her jar."

"Hannah?"

Hannah turned her curious gaze from the woman up to her father. "I think she needs it, Daddy."

Adam weighed the scene. Other customers passed by, entirely uninterested in the dramatic episode playing out. Now behind him stood Lauren, stroller in tow, salty tears gathering but not yet falling underneath her wide eyes. He shrugged his shoulders at her and silently asked, *Well?*

She answered back with a shrug of her own. Her lips said nothing, but the now-dripping tears and melting mascara answered well enough.

"Merry Christmas, ma'am," he said, pulling Hannah to her feet.

"Sir?" The confused woman asked.

"Merry Christmas," he said again, taking Hannah's hand and leading his family back to their vehicle. Without speaking, they loaded back up.

After hearing the final buckle from behind, Adam started the van and twisted his hands on the faded leather steering wheel cover. "What just happened?"

Adam asked, more rhetorically than anything. "Did we just give away Christmas?"

"Yes, dear," Lauren answered. "We just gave away Christmas."

Adam backed the van out and they rode away in silence.

The Maxwells continued on that afternoon to their traditional department store and agreed to a manageable ten-dollars-per-person budget. With just enough cash between them, Adam and Lauren divided the children and blended into the bustling crowd of last-minute shoppers. They met after just twenty-five minutes and rode home without any discussion of how Christmas morning would have a different—though remarkably familiar—theme.

The next morning the children awoke to the aroma of cookies baking and hot chocolate. Over their once-a-year treat breakfast, Adam and Lauren explained that though they were very proud of Hannah's noble act of charity, they could not afford to replace the Christmas funds. "This year," they said, "will be different." Then they opened a few gifts from both grandmas and grandpas, one each from Uncle Steven and Aunt Terri, and the humble gifts purchased for one another.

After they finished opening the packages, Adam asked Lauren to share one thing she loved about Hannah and each of the twins. She did, and then added a tender note about her well-meaning husband. Adam returned the gesture, telling Hannah how proud he was of her bravery and sensitivity to others, and praising Lauren for her knack for maintaining such beauty—inside and out. Hannah caught the vision and wanted her own turn. She gushed genuine "I love yous" to everyone and thanked her dad for not being mad.

"About what, princess?" He pulled her onto his lap.

"About giving away Christmas."

After clearing the modest mess of paper and bows, the family spent some time playing games together, and Adam queued a family video of the twin's second birthday. They later shared stories and jokes until the spirit of the day was unlike any the Maxwells had experienced since they began living as a family of two.

That night was spent with most of the aunts

and uncles in town, congregating at the home of the in-laws, Frank and Dora. Adam and Lauren swore Hannah to secrecy, bribed her with extra marshmallow fudge, and agreed—at least for the time being—to keep their Christmas Eve adventure private.

In the car on the way home, with all three little girls in deep sleep behind them, their parents debated a new tradition. Neither needed convincing. A new jar reappeared on the twenty-sixth and slowly filled with change during the remaining winter months. No games and no gimmicks to fill it faster than through the normal accumulation of daily pocket change. By Memorial Day it was half full, already with a few bills mixed in to save space. By December it was loaded airtight.

On Christmas Eve they secretly gave the jar to one of Hannah's teachers who'd been laid off that summer in a budget consolidation and was struggling with her checkbook and self-confidence.

The next year's jar went to a wealthy furniture client who hardly needed the money but who they privately surmised might appreciate his own lesson in giving. They noticed the countenance of the longtime curmudgeon brighten in the coming visits. They suspected he had given the jar right back away to someone in more financial need.

One night at a romantic restaurant, while the girls spent the evening being spoiled at Grandma's, Lauren leaned across the table and asked, "Hon, how often do you think about the Christmas Jar?"

"Every time I empty my pockets," he answered, twirling his salad fork. "Every single time."

She kissed the back of his calloused hands.

ELEVEN

Adam took a long drink from the lemon ice water Lauren had prepared without anyone noticing. Hope sat on the floor, her legs pulled towards her, her chin resting on her blue-jean knees. This time it was Hannah's turn to interrupt Adam's long breath. "I love that story, Daddy," she said, her head resting in her husband's lap.

"You always have," he answered richly. "And why not? You're the star."

"No, Dad, *you're* the star." She stood and walked to his chair. She bent forward and wedged her arms around him and between his broad back and his brown cloth recliner.

"Kissing booth!" one of the twins called, and before

Hope could blink twice, the entire Maxwell family was swarming Adam and kissing his cheeks and forehead.

"Hope, save me!" he called in mock alarm. But the puckering only intensified, and the sight nearly paralyzed her. A melancholy cloud settled and Hope faded out and into her own living room. Instantly she was back on her flower-patterned couch on the night she held her mother and kissed her good-bye for the very last time. After fifteen or twenty seconds of the joyous banter, the noise settled, and Hope's thoughts collected back into her own jar.

"This . . . is . . . amazing." She looked to Adam. "Your story, and all those jars over the years. It's inspiring. That's what it is." Hope considered that she might actually have more questions now than when she first knocked on their door.

"Inspiring? That might be overreaching, but it's been a blessing, to be certain."

"A blessing for the woman at the bank, for Hannah's teacher, and all the others you've helped."

"Sure, but it's also a blessing for Hannah, and for the rest of us. The jar isn't about money."

"I'm still listening." At this Hope was becoming an expert.

"You've heard the saying 'It's the thought that counts'?"

"Of course."

"It couldn't be more true than in this case. The money has never been enough to save anyone. But every day we notice that jingling in our pockets and purses, and that saves *us*. I guess it's a daily remembrance of sacrifice. Not a day passes when we don't think of—"

"The Christmas Jar," his family answered in unison, like members of a well-trained choir. Laughter again filled the room, and while the others struck up conversations of their own, Hope sat still, first staring into space, then at her feet tucked beneath her. She reflected on the letters she'd found in the paper and then read a hundred times. She replayed the night her own jar arrived. She relived last year's trip to Chuck's for an excruciating solo Christmas Eve dinner.

"Hope?" Lauren sat down next to her and placed an arm over her sagging shoulders. Hope wiped her eyes and nose and lifted her head. "Honey?"

"Excuse me." Hope cleared her throat. "I'm sorry, I really did *not* see this coming."

"What's the matter?" With Hope's eyes closed, Lauren almost sounded like her own mother.

Hope was awash with emotions she'd primarily held in storage since Louise's initial diagnosis. For over two decades, Louise had epitomized to her daughter a strong-spined woman. And though generous and kind, Louise rarely let her emotions show. Only Hope had ever witnessed her mother shed her rugged blue collar, and even then it was only within the sacred walls of their home. Hope could count on one hand the number of times Louise had cried tears of her own.

Hope felt conflicting pride for endearing herself to this family. Unbelievably, she'd arrived at the point where she might have turned to Lauren and called her "Mom" without the faintest hint of overstepping any bounds.

"Hope?" Lauren called again, and her eyes ordered the others in the room to vanish.

The two sat across from each other on a muted burgundy Persian rug. Hope began in slow and deliberate fashion, but with each chapter of her life her cadence quickened and her tongue loosened. She unfolded the story, beginning with her introduction to the world at Chuck's Chicken 'n' Biscuits on U.S. Highway 4. She ended with a tearful and painstakingly vivid account of a solemn night at home the previous winter when her mother quietly slipped away.

Regretfully omitted was any mention of the Christmas Eve burglary and the appearance of her very own Christmas Jar, the nearly completed story scheduled soon for the *Daily Record* front page, and the unsettling concoction of guilt and acceptance settling in Hope's stomach.

TWELVE

Though Hope's questions had been answered, and the origin of the Christmas Jar was now part of her own personal history, she continued stopping by the Maxwell home at least once a week for another month. Relieved, Hope no longer needed to invent thinly veiled excuses. She simply enjoyed being there, and that was enough for her second adoptive family.

Late one Saturday afternoon, Hope announced that her senior project was nearing an end. "You won't have me to kick around much longer, I'm sorry to say." But even as she said it she knew the desire to be around Adam, Lauren, and their affable children would be impossible to ignore. In a peculiar way Hope never envisioned, thoughts of one day saying good-bye guaranteed a case of serious nausea.

"I'd like to read it, provide some feedback," Adam offered yet again as Hope donned her jacket and gathered her notes. He'd been offering for weeks to read her research paper and provide "constructive criticism." "Construction, that's what I do, you know."

"I know," she answered again. "But I'm real self-conscious, you know that." Hope winked good-bye, and he blew a dusty kiss in return. "Next time, my favorite carpenter." Then she left, wishing as she had for months that she didn't have to.

Hope rose every morning at five to work on her magnum opus. Her feature had already grown into a two-part story, covering not only her own experiences but also those of four thankful writers whose letters had run in the paper. But the highlight, and the headline, belonged to a close-knit local family full of life, enamored with wood, and in love with Christmas. They were the genesis of the jars that redefined the meaning of the holidays. The headline was already chosen: "Christmas All Year Round."

Through the final weeks of her "investigation," as she referred to it at the paper, Hope skillfully developed a theory that the Maxwells' inevitable negative reaction to her article would be muted by the positive publicity. In a weekly meeting with Lyle and another senior editor she even uttered the phrase "win-win."

They might be reluctant heroes, she thought. *But they're still heroes . . . and the world loves heroes.*

One summer evening, with her husband, Dustin, and a brother-in-law off at a late movie, Hannah walked Hope through the steps of refinishing a seriously water-damaged German shrank. Hope sat on a tall swiveling stool, watching with genuine interest as Hannah, the future of the company, sat on a square, flat dolly alongside the now stunning piece of furniture. She gingerly screwed into place pieces of replica silver antique hardware.

The two giggling women swapped embarrassing little-girl memories until the only light still on in the Maxwells' quiet neighborhood was hanging above their heads, casting shadows across an unfinished restoration project.

"If I could have chosen a big sister," Hope said, "it would have been you."

"And, hey, I would trade those silly kid sisters of mine faster than you can sand a Popsicle stick."

"I'm serious. You—and your folks—even the twins—have been so good to me. I'd give about anything for a sister like you."

"You're nuttier than Jimmy Carter's pantry," Hannah ribbed. "You *have* a sister like me." She craned her head around to meet Hope's eyes. "How is it possible," she added, turning again to her work, "that a research paper for school could have delivered you so perfectly into our family?"

"Fate," Hope answered, wishing it were true.

Hope drove away that night, as she had on so many others, imagining the day her story would put an end to her career as a small-town newspaper girl. But she knew that very same day's schedule also called for a difficult conversation with the family that had opened their home, and their hearts, to a gregarious, aggressive, and increasingly flawed young woman and college student.

THIRTEEN

Congratulations, Hope," Brandi the classifieds secretary called as Hope grabbed two messages from her box along the long wall separating her old department from a modestly sized break room.

"Thanks?" Hope replied in the tone that meant she had no idea what she'd missed.

"The profile. You didn't know?"

"Profile? It's Monday, help me out, would you, Brandi?"

"You are the *Daily Record* featured staffer of the month. Come on, now, you didn't know?"

Hope's face turned ashen. "No, I . . . had no clue."

"Just between you and me, I think Mr. Butler

might have kept it quiet, thinking you'd talk them out of it."

"You can say that again." Dizzy and fighting for at least one good breath, Hope bypassed her usual glory walk through the downstairs desks and fast-walked to the stairs and to her second-floor station with the leather desk pad.

Already sitting there, cut from the paper and mounted on white foam board, was a copy of the 750-word profile of up-and-coming associate editor Hope Jensen. It chronicled her career at the paper from her days as a high school intern through three well-deserved promotions. It honored her ability to wear many hats at once. It touched on her unique upbringing, her three-year college career and early graduation, and her proven ability to overcome obstacles. It closed with a subtle mention of a "current investigation with career-defining promise."

Hope finished reading the article and rested her head on her desk. It was 8:45 A.M. *There are options,* she convinced herself. *I could jet there, break every speed limit between here and the Maxwells', and pull the paper from the front step before they see it.* She looked again at the clock on the wall. Eight forty-six. At that hour, on a sun-drenched Monday, Hope knew there was no chance the paper hadn't already been retrieved. *But have they read it?* She spun ideas, stretching and reaching in a thousand directions to find a story or clever explanation for why she'd deceived them.

"How's this for an angle?" she said with her head still flat on her desktop. "I am a fraud." The day she had always planned to control, to spin in her favor, had come without warning.

The next and obvious options were difficult to envision. She might sit them down and rationalize her motives; beg for forgiveness; offer to spike the unprinted story; but none of these was palatable. Instead, Hope judged, she would allow time to do the healing. *It worked with Mom, so why not now?*

All morning Hope withstood a barrage of well-meaning pats on the back. "Way to go!" some said. "You've really arrived now!" She wanted desperately to enjoy the day—and the attention—but more than anything she wanted to climb down the fire escape outside her window, stop for tacos and chips, and go home to her mother.

All that evening, Hope tightly gripped her cordless phone. Twice she dialed Adam and Lauren's first three numbers, but dread and guilt kept her from dialing the last four. Instead, she paced through her apartment, picturing the wreckage of her break-in just six months earlier, and acknowledging having done to Adam and Lauren precisely what intruders had done to her. She had entered their lives and their personal space. She had violated them. She had robbed them blind.

Tomorrow. Hope spent the night on the couch, staring at a photo of her and her mother strapping on matching helmets for a bike ride when Hope was an innocent fourth-grader.

The next morning Hope ate oatmeal and spun the phone on the table. She prayed it would ring, knew it wouldn't, and left for work an hour late.

One week turned into two, then three, and four Mondays later the paper was featuring another all-star member of the *Daily Record* family. Hope immersed herself in work, even volunteering to attend an out-of-town conference: "Achieving Circulation Growth through Better Writing." Five days later she returned to work and the same empty feeling of betrayed trust.

A second month passed without a phone call either to or from the Maxwells. With no conscious effort, Hope's smoldering remorse became indignation. *Why haven't they called? Hannah, at least Hannah should have called by now, checked on me. Have they forgotten?*

Twelve weeks ticked by, and a historically hot summer mercifully gave way to Labor Day. Then, on a late-September fall afternoon, Hope drove down the Maxwells' street, stopped just past their house, and watched in the rearview mirror as two men gingerly unloaded from a truck an obviously heavy armoire with one badly damaged door. Lauren observed from the driveway, like a nervous mother, camera in hand to record its condition on arrival. Hope imagined Adam inside his shop, preparing a space, sweeping away the remnants of their last success. With the deliberation of a heart surgeon, he would choose his instruments, arrange the lights, and say a silent prayer.

Hope pulled away and watched in her rear-view mirror until trees and other houses obstructed Restored, Inc. from view. She knew that the Maxwells were long over their sure disappointment. She'd not hurt them, damaged their business, or left them scarred in any tangible way. It had been a simple breach of trust—nothing more.

Meandering through light weekend traffic, Hope realized that as difficult as reappearing would be, she could not hide forever. Not only did she need the Maxwells back in her life, but her conscience ached for their forgiveness.

After deliberating over much less dramatic scenarios, Hope chose a grand holiday homecoming. The prodigal daughter would return on Christmas Eve, just after her early annual dinner at Chuck's Chicken 'n' Biscuits. She would come with her own full jar, her symbolic peace offering. Standing bravely on the porch, she would look Adam in the eye and ask for forgiveness. Then one by one she'd apologize to Lauren, who'd offered such warmth and kindness; then to the twins, who accepted her with genuine friendship; and finally to Hannah, who in such a short time became the sister the orphan from Chuck's never had.

She would also present a professionally framed copy of her first front-page feature. They would read it. They would finally understand.

————————

Thanksgiving approached, and Hope rebuffed a deluge of dinner invitations. They came from her Uncle Bob, her mother's only sibling; Lyle and his wife; and a few single friends from the paper. But the poster child workaholic trudged straight through the holiday without a sniff of turkey and stuffing. Instead, she stayed on top of deadlines and immersed herself in work.

December delivered the first significant snowfall and the red, green, and gold glows of holiday décor that always followed. Though her own Christmas spirit was dampened by another year without her mother and the mounting anxiety of a reunion with the family she'd left behind, Hope's own Christmas Jar was filling fast. She sincerely looked forward to giving away her very first. In her never-resting conscience, her jar was set to play an important role in the process of forgiveness and starting over.

FOURTEEN

The loud ring just inches from her ear startled Hope and sent her just-toasted plain bagel toppling to the desktop. It was fifteen minutes to eight on a bitterly cold December morning. She was treasure hunting for a strawberry jam packet through the desk of a former community page co-worker, Janelle Roberts.

"Good morning, the *Daily Record*." It was déjà vu, taking her back to her days downstairs as a lowly ad writer.

"And to you. I have an obituary to run. Have I reached the right department?"

"Yes, but—"

"No one answered the main number, so I followed

the auto-attendant to this extension." The man's voice was pleasant, quiet—but confident.

"I am sorry for the trouble, but I don't believe the operator is in until eight. I can take a message, though, if you—"

"Not necessary. I have something prepared. I can quickly read it—"

"Gotcha," Hope said, discovering a packet of jam under a replacement roll of Scotch tape.

"Excuse me?"

"I'm sorry." She recovered. "I meant yes, I'd be happy to take it down."

"Appreciate it. Whenever you're ready."

Hope set aside her bagel and jam packet, reached for a pad and pencil, and sat on the edge of the desk.

"Go ahead, sir."

"'On December eighteenth,'" the man began, "'devoted father, husband, and successful area business-man Adam Maxwell died of a heart attack while working on his latest antique furniture restoration project at his home studio.'"

Hope's own heart stopped. "I'm sorry, who?" Hope

stood, and her heart took off again, jumping to her throat.

"Adam Maxwell, an area businessman and my father-in-law." Hope finally recognized the voice. It was Hannah's husband, Dustin.

Hope grasped for the chair and sat. She looked around the room for a sign that this was just another inexplicable dream being played out at four A.M. from the couch in her apartment.

"Miss?" the man called. "Are you there?"

She took four quick bursts of air into her lungs. "Yes, yes," she answered.

"You knew him?"

She heard the words, but her churning mind ground them into sounds she could not understand. She stared at the notepad and saw tears bypassing her face and falling straight to the yellow page below.

"Hello?"

"I'm sorry, Dustin," she whispered and hung up the phone.

The fiercely independent and never unprepared young woman sat broken in a lump of disbelief, tears running down both cheeks to the corners of her mouth. She left the bagel and jam where they sat on Janelle's desk, slowly took her feet, and walked toward the front door and to her car. Whether she passed anyone, whether they greeted her or expressed any concern, Hope would never know.

She opened the back door to her vehicle, climbed in, and lay in the back seat. Her body heaved and shook as she cried the deep, scarring tears that only death brings.

It took the better part of an hour for Hope to regain her equilibrium and feel confident enough to step from the vehicle and walk back across the parking lot without losing her way and collapsing. She successfully navigated her way to the first-floor restroom, rinsed her face with cool tap water, and stared at the picture of grief in the dirty mirror. The woman she saw was familiar. She was the woman who'd lost a parent before.

Hope left the empty women's restroom, fetched her purse, told a colleague upstairs she needed to run a quick errand, and disappeared for the day. From her

apartment she phoned Janelle at her desk and asked if
a gentleman had called that morning with an obituary.

"Hey, Hope," Janelle greeted her. "Yes, there was
a message from a guy on my phone saying he'd started
to dictate a family obit and someone hung up on him.
That was you?"

"Sort of. Sorry 'bout that. I'll explain later."

"You okay? You sound a little roughed up."

"I feel a little roughed up." She thought the phrase
a perfect fit. "Could you read it to me?"

"Sure, Hope. One sec."

She stopped pacing and sat on the futon couch in
her living room.

"'On December eighteenth, devoted
father, husband, and successful area business-
man Adam Maxwell died of a heart attack
while working on his latest antique furniture
restoration project at his home studio. He was
fifty-eight. Together with his wife of thirty-six
years, Lauren Chapin Maxwell, they operated
Restored, Incorporated, a highly respected

local company known to many readers. Mr.
Maxwell founded the enterprise during college
and has never held any other jobs, many times
forgoing expansion to keep the operation small
and home based. In addition to his involve-
ment with his church and many local charities,
Mr. Maxwell has sponsored his daughter's soft-
ball teams long since the end of their playing
days. Mr. Maxwell was a loving and witty husband, a brother, and a wonderful father. He is
survived by his wife; three daughters, Hannah
(Dustin) and twins Clara and Julie; and three
siblings, Steven, Terri, and Jeff. Funeral ser-
vices will be held at noon, December twenty-
fourth, at Wood and Hill Mortuary at 104
South Main Street.'"

What she had prayed was a dream, a joke, or a
simple misunderstanding now crushed her already fragile psyche.

"Someone you know?"

"You might say that."

"Sorry to hear. Anything I can do?"

"Actually, yes. Connect me to Lyle upstairs, could you please?"

"You got it. Hang on."

After the usual series of clicks and pops, Hope spent several mostly composed minutes conveying the sad news.

"That's a tough one, Hope." Lyle had been long aware of her relationship with the family and her consternation at his running the surprise profile on her in the paper. "I'm sorry for you."

For me? Hope reeled. She thought of the family gathering in their humble home and preparing to bury their patriarch. *For me?* The unspoken question and answer were obvious to everyone else. Hope's Christmas Eve homecoming had been canceled.

FIFTEEN

Hope spent the afternoon driving circles around the suburbs, debating, deciding, and reconsidering whether to stop at the Maxwell home. She drove by, and seven or eight unfamiliar cars lined the street. The garage door, usually open to reveal a storm of sawdust and energy, was closed tight.

She drove by a second time, parking four houses away on the opposite side of the street. She laid her seat down as far as it could go and lost herself looking up into the sagging gray fabric above. Then she turned her head to the right and saw a healthy image of her mother, also lying back in her passenger seat and staring up. The view was familiar.

Hope's high school graduation gift had been a

years-in-the-making road trip to Washington, D.C., and a tour of the *Post* arranged by her high school senior English teacher. Hope and her mother were wowed by the size and scope of the newspaper's headquarters and the controlled chaos that buzzed from room to room. The starstruck visitors breathed in a thousand memories and after three nonstop days headed home. But Hope knew one day she'd be back for more than just sightseeing.

After a half day on the road, Louise suggested the two pull off at a rest stop. They laid their seats back as far as they could go, and Hope told her mother dazzlingly vivid stories of her road ahead until Louise pulled a coat over herself and dozed off.

After a few more minutes of gazing across the front seat, in a car now parked on the Maxwells' street, Hope finally conceded her mother wasn't really there. The seat was empty. And instead of an eighteen-year-old young woman with limitless and untapped potential grinning from the driver's seat, there lay a lost mid-twenties reporter still weighted by mostly untapped potential and two gaping holes in her soul.

Hope repositioned her seat, took the wheel in her hands, and felt an unmistakable urge to recompose the surreal scenes of her life. She started her car and, as she pulled away, watched the shrinking pictures in her rearview mirror. "Time for one more story."

Within an hour she was sitting at her kitchen table writing in longhand. Each sentence exploded off the page, expanding and filling space until the story felt whole. She once would have traded everything to have her masterpiece plant her firmly on journalism's front lines and on the *Daily Record's* front page. But now she cared only that it planted her back on the muted burgundy Persian rug on the floor of the Maxwells' living room. And she'd trade everything for that.

Three days later, on Christmas Eve, Hope arose early and retrieved the special Christmas edition of the paper from a box in the parking lot of her apartment complex. Dressed in baggy flannel shorts and a sweatshirt, Hope unfolded the paper to view the front page, holding it tightly with both hands and standing in the glow of a streetlight.

"Christmas Jars and Hope." The byline put goose

bumps on the back of her neck: "by Hope Jensen." The long-awaited moment, one dreamt of since her years as a bubbly middle schooler, the one she'd lived in her mind a million times since her mother left, was finally at her doorstep. But it was nothing like what she had imagined. Missing was the beaming woman and her sheet cake, thoughtful embraces, and the hurrahs that accompany such achievement. In their place sat a lonely girl on a yellow curb, oblivious to the cold and the wind whipping her bare legs. The brightest moment in her brief but stellar career was passing not in triumph but as painful redemption.

Hope read the piece silently. As she finished reading, she leaned back, allowing in deep, cleansing breaths of thin morning air that filled and stung her lungs. She folded the paper neatly and walked with a forgotten bounce back up the stairs to her warm apartment. She prepared and ate a bowl of oatmeal with blueberries, her mother's favorite.

She dressed warmly, picked up her change-filled jar, and set off to experience for the first time the miracle of blessing someone other than herself.

With tender care, as if it were an unwitting baby, Hope wrapped the jar and belted it into the passenger seat next to her. She drove first around the edge and then through the middle of town, at last settling on a well-used downtown park. She stood in front of her car, positioned between her headlights, scanning dawn's landscape for a worthy yet safe target. Coming across and into the light from her left was a middle-aged man struggling to push a metal shopping cart across the loose-gravel path. Hope thought him too young to be living on the street.

She waited until he was exactly in front of her, some fifteen feet ahead, and very well lit by the bright beams of light from behind. "Sir, Merry Christmas."

The man didn't respond, and for the first time she questioned the wisdom of a young woman stopping a vagrant on a dark gray morning in a public park.

"Merry Christmas," she repeated. He nodded his head and worked to maneuver his cart around her. She thrust the jar at him as he tried to pass. He stopped.

"I'd like you to have this," she blurted.

His eyes found the jar but his hands stayed firmly

on the cart's handle. "Really, for you." She gestured with it, placing it against his chest. "I'm sorry it's not more."

"Thank you very much, miss," he said meekly. "But I can't."

Hope was frustrated and unprepared. *This is not what I planned for.* "Please, sir, I know it's not very much, but I'd like you to have it."

The man placed both hands around the jar and lifted it up to examine. "Goodness, it's over half full. You should move on. There are certainly others in the park who need this more. Try beyond the bridge . . ."

"Please?" Hope put her hands in front of her, not meaning to beg but at once realizing it might have looked that way.

The man stood motionless, staring at her, warmed at the first person not to avoid his eyes in as long as he could remember. "Thank you. Thank you for this." With care the man placed the jar in the cart and draped it with a thin flannel shirt.

"You're so welcome," Hope answered, fighting a frog in her throat.

Then in a moment Hope would replay for the rest

of her life, the homeless man reached out to hug her. She hesitated just a second too long. First his arms dropped, then his head, and he sheepishly backed away.

"Wait, wait. . . . You're welcome." She stepped in and returned the gesture, wrapping her arms around his broad shoulders. She breathed in deeply, almost choking at the wet smell of mold. It was a smell she hoped never to forget.

SIXTEEN

Hope spent the morning ignoring a dozen phone calls, no doubt from congratulatory and curious friends. Then when her hair, makeup, and muted gray skirt-and-sweater combination were in perfect order, she drove to the funeral of Adam Maxwell.

She arrived earlier than expected and avoided tension by walking a few city blocks around the stately funeral home. Only when she could clearly hear "Amazing Grace" from the mourners inside did she swallow hard, triple-check her purse for tissue, and pull open the giant wooden door. The moment took her back to the first time she had met Adam, one year before.

It was as if someone had known she would arrive

late and not wish to be seen. To her relief, a single folding chair sat deep in the back, half-hidden by long black curtains extending from a track high on the beige ceiling. She settled in, buried her tissue in her trembling lap, and listened to those who loved—and had been loved by—Adam Maxwell.

One after another the children spoke of a greatness defined not by a singular moment or trait but by time. At her mother's request, Hannah, the eldest, delivered the eulogy. She spoke with elegance of her father's love of sanding rough, damaged wood. Slowly he worked at the edges and imperfections. "Dad used to say every morning when he brought the studio to life that no one can rush the process of perfection." She smiled at the twins sitting as statues on the front row on either side of their mother. Lauren spread her arms wide around them, pulling them into her. Just a few feet to their left rested the man they had come to bury.

After Hannah came Adam's two brothers. First the stoic Steven told childhood tales of his older brother's secret kindness. There were hundreds of such acts, he surmised. "But he never took any credit." He finished by praising Adam's unfiltered dedication to family. Steven said that though his brother had a multitude of opportunities to expand the family enterprise into a large-scale commercial operation, Adam steadfastly refused. "We're not in this for that kind of success," he was fond of saying.

Terri, the only sister, then spoke of Adam's fierce protection of his "favorite sister." She finished through controlled crying: "When Dad died, Adam became the guy in my life I could run to. He knew me, and when nobody else 'got me'"—she gestured the quotes with her index and middle fingers on both hands—"Adam did."

JJ concluded the program with more of a comedy routine than a tribute, but the mourners enjoyed every embarrassing family story and impersonation of Adam. "My brother used to say I was always performing, and he was right. But today, big brother, this is no performance at all." He turned to the casket. "I will miss you, I will cherish your name, and I will always love you. Now, get back to work on your latest project already, would you?" He bent over and kissed the casket. "Good-bye," JJ said. But only those on the front row heard.

The funeral lasted ninety minutes. Hope memorized thousands of details to record later in the unfinished scrapbook her own mother left behind. She left during the closing number, a soaring duet by sister Terri and JJ's glowing, beautiful wife, Randa. Standing outside the funeral home, Hope listened to every note and hurried off to her car when a chorus of simultaneous "Amens" ended the service.

Sitting in her car, hidden away on a one-way side street, Hope marveled at how quickly the headlight procession developed and began moving down the street and toward the cemetery. She had decided days before she would join its tail end and watch from a distance, without joining the graveside gathering. Parked far enough away, and with her windows rolled up, she watched the ceremony unfold.

As the service ended, Hope could see that the small items loved ones placed on his casket just before they returned to their cars were paintbrushes, carving tools, and sheets of sandpaper. Every inch of Hope wanted to be there, to touch the casket before it was slowly lowered six feet. But her presence would distract, she decided, and might be the final nail she could not bear.

Hope pulled away long before Lauren and the immediate family were loaded into the two limousines and embarked on the journey home. There, Hope would be waiting on their front porch, where she prayed her own restoration might begin.

———·———

Hope's legs shook as she took the five steps from the sidewalk to the Maxwell front porch. She sat on the top step, faced the street, covered her legs with her jacket, and pondered her future with—and without—forgiveness. She counted passing cars, noted more than a handful that seemed to slow and drive on, and noticed a plastic bag lying well right of the front door. Its nose hung over the farthest edge of the porch. From her spot she could tell it was the day's unread edition of the *Daily Record.* Her mind calculated the impact of the family's not having read it before her homecoming with Lauren and the girls.

Thirty minutes passed. Then with imagined but building music in the background, the two limousines rounded the corner and rolled to a graceful stop. Hope stood, letting her coat fall to the side, and for a moment would not have felt the cold if the temperature were twenty below.

In unison JJ and Steven exited from the front passenger seats of each car and opened the oversized back doors. Their wives stepped out first, oblivious to the stranger waiting like a courier at the front door. Then came the twins, one from each car, and a few children Hope wished she knew. Then from the second, out stepped Hannah and Dustin.

Hope had anticipated and now fought the searing urge to jump into the bushes to her left, over a neighbor's fence, and well out of sight. "Patience," she thought she heard her mother whisper in the afternoon wind. "Patience."

It seemed an eternity until Dustin reached back into the car and tenderly pulled Lauren into view. At the sight of her, Hope found that her controlled breathing gave way to hiccups.

"Mother," Hannah said softly, taking her widowed mother by the arm. "Is that . . . is that Hope?"

Hope tried to lift her hand to wave but could not move it.

While Hannah led her mother through the chatting family and toward the porch, the younger children asked for and received permission to play. Hope's eyes locked onto the children as a game of tag erupted and finally spilled around the house and into the backyard. Looking back to the street, she was startled to see Hannah and Lauren now standing one step below her.

"Where have you been, young lady?" Lauren said.

But before Hope could concoct a snappy retort, Lauren's arms reached forward in a swift movement and enveloped Hope inside and out. The tears Hope had kept at bay all day now poured at full volume, and the heavy sobbing that only comes with true remorse filled the air.

"Come, come, my dear," Lauren said, stroking her back. "*I'm* the widow here." Hope laughed, let go, let Lauren kiss her wet cheeks and move on to the door. "Inside everyone, it's Christmas Eve."

Hannah stepped aside as the others moved onto the porch and through the door. When the last straggler shut the door behind him, Hannah looked to Hope, now pulling tissue from her coat pocket. "It's good to see you, Hope." The simple words brought music again in the background that only Hope could hear.

"I am *so* glad," she answered, stepping forward and wrapping her arms around Hannah. "I missed you."

"We missed you, too," said Hannah.

"We?" Hope released her arms.

"Yes, *we*. You disappeared on all of us, you know."

"I know, and I need you to know how sorry I am. This has weighed on me, eaten at me, for so long I can't—" The tears returned, and Hannah embraced her again.

"Shhh. It's all right." Hannah's hand cradled Hope's head.

"I wanted so badly to apologize to your dad," her voice shook.

"I don't know how to tell you, Hope, but that would not have been necessary."

Hope lifted her head and looked Hannah in the

eyes. "Of course it was. I lied. I ran. He was so good to me. You were *all* so good to me."

Hannah pulled her tightly in once more and whispered in her ear. "He never knew." She paused and let the revelation settle. "He never knew."

While they sat and held hands, Hannah explained that when the article ran, highlighting Hope's achievements at the paper, her sisters and their mother agreed to toss it in the neighbor's trash. "Dad never knew," she repeated.

For Hope, the truth was at once both a relief and a crushing burden.

"We thought you'd call, stop by, send a letter, something, anything."

Hope struggled for words but found nothing more than the ones meant mostly for Adam. "I'm sorry."

"I know." Hannah smiled. "You're here, aren't you?"

Hope's well-rehearsed script had taken an impromptu turn that no amount of research or rehearsal could have readied her for. She smiled back and took five long steps to the paper hiding at the far end of the porch. She pulled it from its bag and placed it in Hannah's hands. "Read this," she said, checking the time on her wristwatch. "I've got to go."

"Wait! Stay!" But Hope was already down the stairs and gliding down the sidewalk. "Do you have dinner plans?" she called out, but Hope kept running. "It's Christmas Eve, Hope. Mom wants to see you. *Everyone* wants to see you."

Hope stopped before leaping across the street. "I know," she called back. "It's Christmas Eve, and *yes,* I have dinner plans." With that, she vanished and made the drive beyond the edges of town to Chuck's Chicken 'n' Biscuits.

SEVENTEEN

In traditional Maxwell holiday fashion, Lauren and her family spent Christmas Eve eating. This year, instead of Lauren's renowned cooking, they worked through mountains of food left by neighbors and friends in the days since Adam's death. The twins created a list of those needing thank-you cards, and the men gathered in the garage to unwind and decompress from the emotionally draining day.

After the late lunch, Hannah gathered everyone in the same living room where Adam once eloquently painted for Hope the story of the Christmas Jar. Hannah called order, holding in her hands the Christmas Eve edition of the *Daily Record.* "Given the funeral and all, I assume no one's had time for the paper, right?" Tired heads nodded around the room. "I thought so. Listen, gang, I know this has been a tough day for us, but you might find this interesting. It's the top story."

She turned the paper around and waved it from left to right until everyone had seen the oversized, larger-than-life headline. Then she read it anyway. "'Christmas Jars and Hope, by Hope Jensen.'"

Hannah read each word and the building sentences deliberately, as if answers to their grief were hidden somewhere in the lines.

> (December 24)—A good man has died; his name was Adam Maxwell. Know this, readers, Adam was more rare than a bad meal at Chuck's Chicken 'n' Biscuits, tucked six miles from town on Highway 4.
>
> This reporter first met Adam this past March. We met one evening, along with his elegant bride, in their modest but comfortable, even heavenly, living room. To him I was an eager college student seeking answers from a

successful entrepreneur. Adam was a husband and father willing to teach at every opportunity fate dropped at his size-12 feet.

Days became weeks and weeks grew into months that I strangely both cherish and regret. The man who opened his home, his business, his family, and his heart to me was a giant. Connecting body to soul were veins filled with the warmest, most sincere and honest energy I have ever known. In every moment, in every decision, in every step on his journey Home, he was a man of refreshing openness and honesty. As for me, unfortunately, I have been less so.

Most longtime subscribers will not recognize my name, but my voice has been a small part of this paper since my senior year of high school. Forever the nerd, I passed on after-school activities, parties, and cruising for boys on Friday nights up and down Grande Blvd.

Rather, I embedded myself in this paper, starting as an intern, moving to classifieds, then community, then editorials, and finally upstairs as a trusted member of the team responsible for every word on these wafer-thin pages. I ran with blind ambition and a deep-seated desire to have you read this very article, positioned prominently on my world's most precious real estate: the front page.

One year ago I was among a handful of unlucky local residents burglarized on Christmas Eve. Seeing your home dismantled and defiled is something indescribable, even to someone who fancies herself good with a pen. But it wasn't what I missed that most changed me. It was what I found.

During the shuffling in and out of my apartment that memorable night, an anonymous angel left a jar filled with coins and a few 20-dollar bills. On it was inscribed: "The Christmas Jar." I found no name and no explanation. It is ironic that this reporter embarked on such an important mission with so few facts. Over the ensuing days I became obsessed with knowing who had been so kind to me and why.

I wanted to thank them in front of you. I wanted to change minds and lives about the meaning of Christmas. The painful reality is that I just wanted to be seen—and read.

My overzealous and misguided energy led me to the introduction that brings these words to your doorstep this morning. Yes, readers, a good man has died; his name was Adam Maxwell.

Since that December evening one year ago, a blessed mystery has unfolded, and great is the temptation to unravel every detail for you. But I shall not. Suffice it to say that despite my best denials, the spirit of the jar has affected me, too.

Though I cannot know how many have been similarly affected by the Christmas Jar tradition, I sense the number is impressive. I suspect many of you today will take jars you've kept tucked away in your homes and deliver them to someone in need. Those needs will vary from social to emotional and, of course, to financial.

The decision about whom to bless will be made in private ways and in private places. Some will gather around kitchen tables later this morning; others will kneel in prayer on soft living room rugs. Some will not decide until the car seemingly stops itself beside some lonely wanderer.

In the days that come, neither givers nor receivers will discuss their experiences beyond the walls of their homes. But by week's end, and without much fanfare, someone will wash a new jar, cleaning it until it sparkles and reflects his or her kind countenance. Then with caring hands this person will wipe it dry and place it in its familiar spot.

That night, one by one, family members will empty their pockets and delight at the clink of change hitting the empty glass bottom. Most days will yield a quarter, a dime, perhaps two nickels and a stray penny. Occasionally Mother will make change for herself by dropping in a worn dollar bill and pulling out an appropriate combination of cool silver coins.

Over the months that follow, the gathering change will leave no recognizable void. Occasionally the temptation to borrow for laundry, a movie, or the ice-cream truck will float through the house, over the jar, and out the back door. But it never lands. The money is spoken for.

Over the course of twelve months these jars will fill slowly but with purpose. Every day, if only for an instant, the benefactor will consider Christmas. For most, including this reporter, there will be a sweet daily reminder of what this day we call Christmas means. Most will pause, if only for an instant, to consider the miracle of a perfect baby boy born in a manger under the brilliant star that predicted it all.

Tonight a grateful single mother, or a homeless man, or a young struggling couple— or perhaps even you—might find such a jar.

You will lift it up and hold it a foot from your wet eyes. You will spin it. You will examine its uncanny beauty. Then you'll wonder why.

The answer is simpler than time and curiosity will tell you. It is not the copper- and silver-colored coins you will empty onto your coffee table. No, the answer is not in the total you will count and put to good purpose in your life. The answer, dear reader, is what went into the jar each day, long before it ever found you.

Friends of the *Daily Record,* I am proud to report that I have discovered the origin of the Christmas Jar. It was a miracle, nothing less, performed by a child, and today made available to all.

May you also find it, and may the spirit of Adam Maxwell live on.

Hannah finished reading, and her face balanced a rare combination of pride, relief, and loss. "I can't believe I made it through that . . ." The room sat in reverence, and before anyone found words, a knock on the door broke the comfortable quiet.

"I've got it," Steven said, slipping off a stool and gliding around the corner to the front door. A moment later he returned with a jar three-fourths full with change. "For you," he said, handing the jar to his mother, who sat snuggled in a blanket in Adam's brown recliner, still taking in the gravity of Hope's front-page feature.

"Amazing," she said, holding it at eye level and spinning it as if seeing a Christmas Jar for the very first time. "Was there anyone there?"

"There was. It was a woman and her son. The boy handed it to me and said, 'Thank you, and God bless.'"

"That's it?"

"That's it."

"Amazing," Lauren said again, and the room hushed around them.

"All right, gang, how about a game?" Hannah slid the paper under her chair for safekeeping.

"Yeah!" one of the older children answered.

"How about"—Hannah paused for effect—"kissing booth?"

The family converged on the matriarch, Lauren, drenching her in wet, loving kisses.

"All right, troops," she begged, "enough! I've got freezing coins dumping all over me!"

They kissed her one last time, and the laughter held on well through the cleanup.

During the next thirty minutes, the sun began its final descent toward the approaching Christmas. A card game sprouted in the dining room, the children gathered around a television in the basement, and Hannah and her mother sat in the living room looking through family albums.

Three loud knocks on the door interrupted them. "Let me," Hannah said, getting off the floor near her mother's chair and walking to the foyer.

Three minutes later the door shut and she appeared carrying yet another jar, this one decorated with bright paints and white ribbon and filled to the top with coins and bills.

"Another?"

"Yes, Mother, another." Hannah set the jar on the reading table at Lauren's side. "For you."

"What did they say?"

"Get this. They said they're first-timers. They found a jar at their door after church last year. They don't even live around here."

"You're kidding. Did you get their name?"

"Now *you're* kidding, Mother. Of course not. They wouldn't say. They just wanted us to know they were thinking of us, that Christmas was different this year than any other, and to thank you."

Just as Hannah took her seat amid the stacks of photo albums, another knock at the door sounded.

"I'll get it," one of the twins called from the kitchen. A few minutes later she too entered the living room, this time carrying not one but two Christmas Jars. One was a small jam jar, still with its lid, the initials "CJ" written on top in marker. The other was a quart-sized plastic jar that smelled of peanut butter.

Tears began dripping from Lauren's cheeks before she even held them. "I don't know what to say," she muttered.

"One is from an older couple that got their own jar a few years ago when their last child moved out of the house. They thought you could use it."

"Oh, my." She was overcome.

"The other is from a family of eight, believe it or not. Their father was laid off two years back, and a jar appeared on their step Christmas morning. It had almost a thousand dollars in cash. They apologized for not doing as well but wanted you to know they were thinking of you." Hannah bent down and kissed her mother's head. "Look how loved you are, Mother."

"And so too your father," she answered.

"Yes, ma'am."

Hannah and her mother sat silently gazing at the jars, each knowing they had not given jars to any of these people personally and wondering to what extent their family tradition had spread. Without a word, they reopened their albums and again examined family photos, mostly of Adam. Fifteen minutes later, two quick knocks stole their attention once again.

"My turn," Adam's sister yelled out just as she arrived at the door. A short, muffled conversation began and ended with a "Thank you" that was loud enough it could have been meant for someone on the other side of the street. She turned back into the house. "Can I get a hand here?"

"On my way, sis," JJ pledged, and the sound of his heavy feet and skipping pace filled the first floor. "Unbelievable!" he shouted. In Terri's arms were three full jars, and two more sat on the porch just outside the door. "What's happening?" He turned to his sister. They delivered the jars to their mother's spot in the living room.

"I only got the story on one," Terri began. "The others just handed them and ran off." She picked back up a midsized jar with five rolls of quarters and at least five one-hundred-dollar bills. "A very good-looking man handed me this one."

"Easy there, honey," her husband said, entering the room behind her.

"Excuse me, a *modestly* good-looking man handed me this." She winked over her shoulder. "He's a single guy, and judging from his suit and overcoat I imagine he's pretty well off. He received a jar four years ago when he really didn't need it. But it awoke something in him, and he said the next year he made his first-ever donation. *Ever!*"

"I don't understand," Lauren interrupted. "Why him? Why us today?"

"I guess some people just need to learn how to give, Mother."

But before Lauren could reply, another knock once again turned their heads from one another to the front door.

"I got it!" JJ, Terri, and Hannah yelled in unison and jostled for position. JJ playfully pulled his sister and niece back by their waists. He arrived first and flung open the door. The others sat quietly preparing to eavesdrop.

"Mother," Hannah called, "you'd better come see this."

Lauren set aside the most recent jar, unwrapped herself from her warm blanket, and walked to the door. Everyone else in the house not already on the porch followed. She appeared in the open door and saw JJ,

Terri, and Hannah flanking the porch, looking out into the yard and street.

Scattered between the first step and as far as a block away were dozens of people carrying jars, all converging on the porch, all wearing tremendous smiles as wide as any Maxwell had ever seen.

"Amazing," Lauren said so quietly that only she heard. A makeshift line formed, and as if in a funeral reception line the strangers worked up the five steps to Lauren to hand over their Christmas Jars. Some shared their own conversion stories, others offered a warm "Merry Christmas, ma'am," and still others said nothing at all. They smiled as they looked into her eyes, placed their jars in her outstretched hands, and walked away to their own Christmas Eve gatherings.

Jars arrived for almost an hour. Each was taken by Lauren, handed to another, and set aside to make room for the next. Each visitor, from the first to the last, received a pure and full "Thank you."

"My heart cannot hold anymore," Lauren said to Hannah as the last family disappeared down the stairs and into the gathering darkness.

"Neither can the porch," JJ cracked.

Using an assembly line, they moved the jars into and throughout the living room and kitchen. No one dared speculate on how much money the jars might contain; they knew it didn't matter. Very little was said, for most were still numb, inside and out, from the remarkable generosity, mostly from people they'd never met in all their years at 316 Oakliegh Hill.

EIGHTEEN

The heart of Christmas Eve arrived, and the children were eventually sent off for baths and pajamas. Others hid away to wrap a few final gifts that had almost been forgotten in Adam's passing. Lauren melted back into Adam's chair and listened to the chatter. Her grateful eyes scanned the room, making mental note of the seemingly endless procession of jars. She marveled at the unique nature of each. The grieving widow was awash with a colorful blend of emotions, especially the beginning pangs of loneliness and longing for Adam. She peered at the chair next to her, the one she had occupied for an entire marriage, and wished she were sitting in it instead.

With the bustle calming around her, and just as

her eyes fell closed for the first time in eighteen hours, another knock startled her. "Hannah? Steven?" she called, but no one answered. "Dustin, dear? You down here?" But he was hiding in the studio, sitting on a workbench, pretending to read the sports page. Mostly he looked around and tried to imagine Restored without Adam.

"No, no, I'll get it," Lauren said to herself, unwrapping once again and walking to the door. She pulled it open to see yet another stranger—a middle-aged woman—holding a jar.

"Hello there," she greeted.

"Merry Christmas, Mrs. Maxwell," the woman answered.

The confused look on Lauren's face was hard to ignore.

"The newspaper article," the visitor prompted.

"Yes, of course. Forgive me, we've had a few unexpected visitors tonight," Lauren said, folding her arms across her chest and rubbing her bare arms. "It's gotten cold."

"Christmas Eve," the woman replied. "It's finally here."

"Indeed. Well, won't you come in?"

"Do you mind? I'm sure it's been a long day for you and your family—"

"Don't be silly. Come." Both women stepped into the rapidly cooling foyer, and Lauren closed the door behind them. "Since you know my name, may I know yours?"

"Marianne." The woman stuck her gloved hand out.

"Pleasure, Marianne." She met the woman's hand and shook. "Call me Lauren."

She led the visitor into the living room and gestured to the love seat. "Sit down, please," she said and settled herself once again in her husband's favorite recliner.

Marianne sat down and glanced around the room at the collection of brimming jars.

"I guess you know why I'm here, then," she said.

Lauren looked at the woman quizzically and smiled. "I think I might."

"I want you to know"—she stood and stepped toward Lauren, reaching to hand her the chilly glass jar—"that this jar saved my life."

"Really? How so?" Lauren accepted the heavy jar, turned it around like all the others in sheer wonder, and rested it in her lap.

Marianne stepped back and retook her seat. "A long time ago—a lifetime ago, it feels like—I was a young woman living around here, and I was given a jar myself."

"A lifetime ago? That's an awfully long time."

Marianne took an extra breath and continued. "You're so right. You see, at the time I was a young, naive newlywed. Sort of new, I guess." Lauren wondered if the woman was telling this story for the very first time. "My husband and I were pretty happy, both working, enjoying, I thought, our first couple of years together."

"I remember those times." Lauren's mind spun back thirty-plus years to the early days of her own marriage.

"My husband traveled a lot, and I was home mostly,

trying to keep things organized, learning how to be a homemaker. He was pretty rough with me, but then I thought overall it was probably good. I was learning to be a wife, you know?"

"Dear, it's never—"

"Yes," she interrupted. "I know that now. It's never all right. But he loved me, and when things were good they were real good. Then three years in or so we got pregnant."

"That's wonderful."

"I wish it had been. He wasn't happy. He didn't want it."

"Didn't want it?"

"He wanted me to 'take care of it,' he said. I broke the news to him over the phone while he was in New York or Detroit or somewhere, I don't even remember. He was pretty upset about it, thought I'd somehow tricked him." Marianne rubbed her face and breathed as if refilling her tank. "He came home and he hit me like he never had. He said if I kept it he'd leave. That he wasn't ready. That I wasn't ready."

Lauren stifled the urge to comfort; she knew after

three decades the woman had either long since healed or buried her pain far beyond the reach of comfort.

"I told him I wouldn't, that I couldn't. We were having the baby, and that we could handle whatever rearranging he thought we needed. He said he'd think about it, and things seemed all right for quite a while, seven months actually. We didn't talk much. He traveled more than ever, but the hitting stopped, and I guess things just seemed okay to me. I always thought it could have been so much worse." Marianne's cadence trailed off, and Lauren could see reflected in her face a life of very hard lessons.

"Then he left," Marianne picked up again, "for a ten-day trip in December to Vegas. I was eight months pregnant. Said he'd be back by Christmas. And on Christmas Eve, first thing in the morning, I get this call that a check bounced. I ran down to the bank, and it was gone. He'd taken everything."

"No, tell me he hadn't." Lauren said the words she was supposed to but already knew the answer.

"Every penny . . . I was horrified. I was scared. I was lost for where to go next. I sat on the curb outside, staring at my bank balance on one of those little white sheets of paper."

Footsteps interrupted the unfolding story. "Mom?" Hannah glided in from the hallway. "Everything okay?"

"Yes, love, everything's fine. Join us."

Hannah sat on the floor at her mother's side and rested her arms across Lauren's legs.

"Go on," Lauren told Marianne.

"You must think I'm crazy, but I needed to tell you this."

"Of course, please, continue. And, oh," she interrupted herself, "this is my oldest, Hannah." Lauren gently patted her daughter's head like a bongo. "Hannah, meet Marianne."

"Hi. Didn't mean to interrupt."

"Go on, dear," said Lauren.

"Well, I sat there in shock and was just, frankly, tired of crying. My life was ending. No education, no husband, and a child in me that I couldn't raise. For the first time in my life I felt like there was no hope. Then this little girl walked toward me, just this little angel, she was."

Lauren suppressed a smile that began in her belly and worked up to the tightening corners of her mouth. Chills spread from her toes to her scalp as she took a long, deep breath. Subtly, she tilted the jar in her lap away from her just enough to steal a glance at the delicately painted letters: "ALM."

"She was carrying that very jar, the one in your lap, but filled with a lot more money, I'm afraid, and she asked me to take it." For the first time, the woman— no longer a stranger—began choking on her words.

Hannah took her mother's hand and squeezed gently.

"The girl sat down by me, slid the jar over, and said I should have it. Then a very concerned dad appeared behind her. This girl, this beautiful little girl, told him I needed it, that I should have it. I cannot describe what I felt, but I remember it today like a movie I've seen a million times, you know?"

"You're doing just fine." Lauren replayed in her own mind the story with equally vivid detail. "It's like we were there."

"The little girl and her dad walked away, leaving

this jar full of money next to me. I tried to get a plate number or a description or something so I could look them up and repay them, but I couldn't see through the tears. I must have sat there for another hour."

"Quite a story," Hannah said, still reeling from hearing this familiar story for the first time from the other side.

"That's not quite it. If you don't mind?"

"Absolutely! Go on!" Hannah and her mother spoke on top of one another.

"I walked into the bank, deposited the money— eight hundred seventy-four dollars, ninety cents."

"Imagine that," said Hannah.

"I moved out during the next two days, moved in with a friend, and thought I'd have time to think things through before the baby came. I didn't. I fought contractions as hard as I could, then delivered her on my girlfriend's couch."

"My!" Lauren covered her mouth.

"I stayed for a day or so to get my legs back. Then I took off."

"With a newborn?" Hannah asked.

"Well, I knew if someone came to see me they'd want to tell him."

"Your husband, you mean?" Lauren asked.

"My husband . . . I talked to a clinic about adoption. I was in no way ready to raise this baby, but they said I'd have to have her dad involved—at least until we proved what kind of man he was . . . so I just left."

"You walked away with the baby?" Hannah asked.

"More like ran. I loaded the baby in my car—no car seat, nothing—and drove out of town. When I was a couple miles out, I stopped, dropped the baby off with an anonymous note, and kept running. And honestly? I mean, it's taken me time to get to this, but it was the smartest decision I ever made."

"I can only imagine," Hannah said, still stunned, suppressing the desire to jump to her feet and pull the stranger into her arms.

"Tracking down a gal from school to stay with wasn't as tough as I thought it'd be," Marianne continued. "I stayed with her a couple months until I figured things out. My mom and dad were gone; it's not like I had all that many choices. So I used what was left of the money and went to hairdresser school. Now I do hair, and I do pretty good. I have my own salon in my house."

"We're so happy for—"

"And how can I forget!" she exclaimed. "I'm married now to a great guy, married ten years, no kids, but he treats me like a queen." She thrust her ring finger at them, smiling proudly.

Even if they'd wanted to speak, Lauren and Hannah didn't have the words. Lauren found herself replaying in her mind Marianne's words: . . . *dropped the baby off with an anonymous note.* At the same time, she recalled the image of a young woman sitting on the Persian rug in this very room and telling her life story—a story that began at a restaurant on U.S. Highway 4.

The three women sat in silence, looking at and into one another, each of them reflecting on what had been shared.

After a few moments, Lauren got up from her chair and pulled her still-stunned daughter to her feet. She stepped to the love seat, extended her hand, and said, smiling warmly, "Marianne, do you like chicken?"

NINETEEN

With Marianne in the passenger's seat and her mother comfortably in the back, Hannah drove through their neighborhood, across the edge of downtown, and out toward the darkness of the surrounding countryside. Their cheerful banter quieted when Hannah turned the car onto Highway 4. It stopped entirely when a yellow and white sign came into view.

Hannah turned into the empty parking lot and pulled up facing the wide plate-glass front window of Chuck's Chicken 'n' Biscuits. The restaurant had been dark, illuminated only by a single light peeking from the kitchen over the chest-high stainless steel order counter. But now the headlights shone brightly through the glass, revealing a young woman sitting alone in the booth that knew her best.

Hannah turned off the car, and after a brief pause, Marianne got out. Lauren moved quickly into the passenger's seat, and the two excited women slunk down in their seats, peering over the dashboard, their nerves quivering.

They watched as Marianne opened the front door of the restaurant and walked past the silent boogie-dancing Santa and the darkened Christmas tree. She hesitated just short of the young woman and turned to look through the window at Hannah and her mother. Over the glare of the headlights she saw their heads scrunched together, their faces barely visible over the dashboard. But she could have seen their smiles from the moon.

Marianne turned back to Hope, walked to the booth, and sat across from her for the first time since leaving her in the very same booth precisely one week shy of twenty-six years earlier. Even from their distance in the empty parking lot, Hannah and Lauren could see them gaze across at one another for some time before Marianne's lips finally moved. At last, they saw Hope pull a tightly folded piece of paper from her coat pocket and slide it across the smooth tabletop.

Through two converging beams of light, a tearful daughter and mother watched another tearful daughter and mother become reunited across a white-flecked altar of forgiveness. Then Lauren and Hannah reverently withdrew.

Through the early hours of that blessed morning, the two newly introduced women, a family once again, became acquainted, each eagerly sharing the events of their lives. They wept as Hope shared the miracle of her adoptive mother, Louise, and that gentle woman's graceful passage through this life and into the next.

Dawn approached, and in the gathering light, Hope made out the green edging on Marianne's baby blue eyes. And as the last corner of the restaurant filled with the redeeming light of Christmas morning, Marianne and Hope could be seen playing tic-tac-toe with tater tots that somehow never cooled.

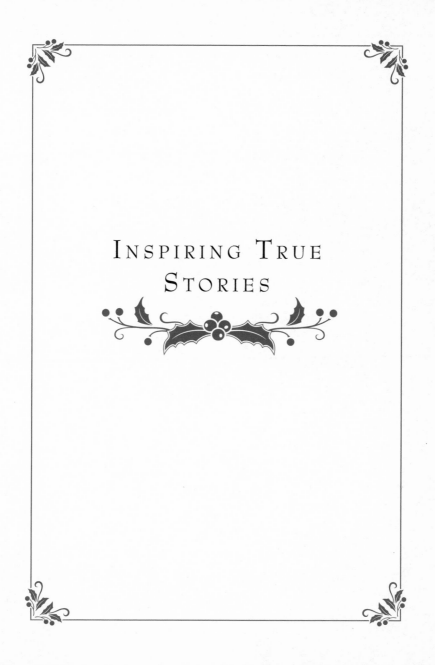

INSPIRING TRUE
STORIES

I BURNT OUR CHRISTMAS

Menan, Idaho

My husband was going to be home and I realized that the fire in the living room was almost out. I didn't want him to have to fuss over the fire, so I grabbed a bag of papers from our bedroom that I had picked up after wrapping what Christmas gifts we had to give to the kids this year, and shoved it into the stove and lit it.

The second that it was engulfed, a wave of panic hit me. My husband's super-generous grandmother had sent gift cards totaling over 300 dollars to us and our children. She usually sends things in pretty Hallmark cards, but this time she sent them in a plain padded manila envelope. Additionally I bought most of the things for the baby from eBay this year, buying them used and trying to save some money. Everything had arrived in yellow envelopes that week, and they all went into the fire.

I burnt our Christmas. Everything under our tree is secondhand garage sale finds. Those gift cards were our fun thing from his wonderful grandma. Those cards represented our only Christmas for my husband and me, but the kids' cards . . .

We are college students with four kids. We had three when my husband got home from Iraq. We knew that it was our only chance to make a change, so we moved halfway across the country and left a lot behind, starting as what felt like the oldest college freshmen ever, but we knew that it would be worth it.

Halfway through the second semester we found out our youngest was going to be joining us. Unplanned, but so welcome was her arrival. We had always wanted another child; our youngest is six and we figured if it hadn't happened already it wouldn't. Her arrival in our family has been so joyous, but the money hasn't been dropping out of the sky.

Then I burnt Christmas last night. I cried, I cursed Christmas, so many emotions went through me.

Honestly I wanted to die. My husband came home from work and took me out to try and find a few last-minute Santa gifts for the kids. We took the baby and left our twelve-year-old home with the other two.

While we were gone, someone left a jar on the steps of our house. It was wrapped in cellophane and a gold ribbon. Inside was your book and just short of 200 dollars in change. They had placed it carefully there for Christmas morning. My twelve-year-old found it. He sees our troubles financially and knew about the missing gift cards.

He knew that those cards were the only way he would be getting anything new this winter, as his wish list has grown to more grown-up toys that we could never afford. He was so sad last night when we left, but he just squared his shoulders and tried to help. He was so happy when we got home. What a gift! He and the two other children didn't touch their miracle jar; they just put it under the tree. Looked at it. Guessed how much change could be in it. Wrote their guesses down. Dreamed about who did it for them. It was such magic in their lives.

Maybe the gift cards can be replaced—I don't know. I do know that the gift left to us by someone restored something in me and my family. I was tired and beaten. My troubles aren't gone, but MY HOPE is restored. Thank you for your book. We will pay it forward.

—JBM

I FELT LIKE A STARVING
STREET PERSON

Clarksville, Tennessee

On Christmas Eve this year, I received an unmarked box on my front doorstep. Inside was a mason jar full of bills and coins. It was simply marked in red and green letters as the "Christmas Jar." Included in the box was a plain wrapped gift. I frantically tore open the gift, hoping to find some clue as to the intent of the jar, and found the book *Christmas Jars*.

Quickly I scanned its cover to find a description of the book and the reason behind the gifts. If I wasn't on medication to prevent me from crying, I would have been shedding tears aplenty as I counted the money. Inside the center of the single one-dollar bills was a hidden one-hundred dollar bill. I felt like a starving street person as I scrounged and sorted the coins. I added up a total of $158.71.

I am a forty-seven-year-old single parent of two, and have been for greater than seventeen years. I don't receive assistance. I work. I am the percentage that makes more than what is needed to qualify for assistance, but still my income is only enough to pay the bills.

I'm unable to finish my story; it has been difficult to explain. Suffice it to say, I would not have been able to buy any presents for my kids without the money in the jar, and I thank this book for the inspiration that encouraged some friend of mine to help me. And honestly, I thank God, because he does hear our prayers and always provides me with exactly what I need!

—Anonymous

MY HUSBAND IS DYING

Hagerstown, Maryland

My husband is dying of leukemia, and one night I was sitting in the bedroom beside him looking at my deceased mother's photo album when I heard the doorbell. When I answered it, nobody was there, but on the doormat was a book with a jar tied to it with a red gingham ribbon. I took it inside and ran to the window to see if I could see anyone outside. I did not. About that time the phone rang and a girl told me to open my door because there was a gift for me and then she hung up. I went back to the bedroom and began reading *Christmas Jars* to find out the meaning of this gift. I was shaking in disbelief that anyone would do such a kind and generous act for us. The next day about noontime, I finally decided to open the jar and count the contents. To my amazement, there was over $500 in the jar! I believe my mother was my angel that night that caused this wonderful act of kindness to come to us. Not knowing how to properly thank an anonymous giver, I decided that the best thing I could do would be to start my own Christmas jar so that next year I can lift someone's spirits the way mine were this Christmas when things were so difficult. It's something I will never forget. God's love did come down at Christmas.

—Peggy

HOW CAN I THANK
WHOEVER DID THIS?

Florissant, Missouri

I'm so blown away right now. It's been a tough year and I almost lost the spirit of Christmas.

Today I woke to finish last-minute shopping. My truck was unlocked and when I got in I found a Christmas jar. I was stunned. When I went across the street to my longtime best friend's house I brought it with me and opened it. It had $200 cash in it and the story!

I will have minor surgery soon and will lose three day's pay. I was so fearful of not being able to pay the mortgage . . . and here was this wonderful miracle. I am humbled by the blessings I have received.

I'm not forcing myself to be in the spirit of Christmas; the spirit is now in me. I am so grateful and humbled. I too will pay it forward. I will collect change all of 2013, and I know so many that are in need to whom I can pass on this wonderful tradition. How can I thank whoever did this? By being a good person and paying it forward. Thank you from my soul whoever you are.

—Nancy

I'M FOREVER GRATEFUL

Logan, Utah

To the group of teenagers at Primary Children's Hospital seven years ago:

On December 12th, 2008, you touched my life for the better. I was surrounded by loved ones in one of the waiting rooms at Primary Children's Hospital when I saw a group of you, just young teenagers, walking through the halls. You were giggling and being a little suspicious. You walked up to me and set a big jar of money on my lap and said "Merry Christmas" before rushing away.

I don't remember how much money was in the jar and I don't remember what all of you looked like. But I do remember the smiles on your faces and how you made me and everyone else in that waiting room feel.

I'll never know why you decided to pick me when you must have walked passed countless others you could have given it to, but I'm forever grateful you chose me.

You didn't know this, but at that very moment, my precious two-day-old baby was undergoing a lifesaving surgery to fix a birth defect. It was a hard and scary day for us, filled with a lot of uncertainty and worry. I want you to know that you were our angels that day. You were our light in the dark and our good in the bad. You turned a negative experience into a positive one. You helped us experience the kind of joy that can only be felt during a hard time.

We were spending our Christmas season in a hospital a couple hours away from home, away from most loved ones, and away from everything else that makes Christmas feel like Christmas, and yet, I've never felt the spirit of Christmas as much as I did that year. You did that for me.

You see, it was never about the money to us. It was about the fact that you made us feel something that no amount of money can buy. You taught us that the gift of service can change a trial into a blessing. I don't think there is anything you can do for another person greater than that.

It's been seven years, but I think about all of you often. I have always wanted to tell you how much your kindness meant to us and how grateful we are for each of you. We have been able to tell many people about your kindness and we pay it forward as often as we can.

The baby that was in surgery that day—his name is Krew, and we are proud to say he is a happy and healthy little boy. Nothing would make us more proud than to see him grow up to be the kind of teenager you were that day. We all know how much the world needs people like you right now. You are the ones that truly make the world a brighter place.

I hope this message somehow finds you, and I sincerely hope that whatever trials have come and will come into your life, you will be blessed in the same way you helped bless us.

—Love, Ashley

BUT THE REAL GIFT
IS THE LOVE

Ogden, Utah

I was standing in the dry storage closet at work, trying to keep the tears back so they wouldn't ruin my mascara. Having smudged eyeliner hurts your tips. It was not just one of those days—it was one of those months.

See, as a twenty-five-year-old divorced woman living alone and waiting tables to pay for college tuition, holidays don't mean family time, they just mean overtime. I had received an email earlier that day informing me that I did not get accepted into my college program and I would have to wait another three months before I could try again. I felt as though the last year of struggling to pay tuition and books and fees had been for nothing. I would have to retake classes and pay for yet another semester trying to pull my GPA up a few fractions of a point. Having my dreams of teaching in a classroom (a career I have always wanted) completely dashed, I tried to pretend that table 52 not having enough chips with their dip or that table 41's preference for no ice, two extra lemons, and a lime with their diet Pepsi was of the utmost importance. And yet the not-so-gentle tone in my manager's voice, a snappy demand from a customer, finding a zero written on the tip line of the check, and getting triple-sat all at once sent me over the edge.

So I stood there in the dry storage trying not to cry—and failing. It took a few minutes but I was finally able to compose myself and finish my shift. Seeing young couples with babies, old married couples, and even a girl I went to high school with . . . all happy, all surrounded by people who loved them, enjoying a meal, was hard. It was hard knowing I would go home to my little place with no festive decorations, no friendly faces, no loved ones. Just alone.

As I pulled into the driveway at two A.M. after closing and cleaning the restaurant, I was so tired I practically tripped as I opened my door. Someone had left a large Christmas tub on my stoop. At first I thought it was popcorn or cookies from my neighbors, but when I lifted it I was shocked at its weight. Sitting down on my stairs, I opened the gift to find hundreds, even thousands, of coins inside with $45 folded up on top, and a book tied to the canister titled *Christmas Jars*.

My breath stopped and for the first time since my divorce, I cried happy tears instead of sad ones. I simply couldn't believe that someone would do something so nice, so much, for me. Sob after sob—I had never been so grateful for spare change. It took several minutes to regain my composure, only to lose it again and again, crying every time I looked at the several pounds of coins sitting next to me on the stairs. I sat there thinking it was all too much. It was simply too big of a gesture; it couldn't have been meant for me. Maybe they had the wrong house. I don't really have any friends, I don't attend a church, and only a few classmates from my study group knew where I lived. And yet . . . there it was propped on my door. It meant I was not alone.

It meant that someone cared enough to spend months collecting change—for me. It meant that I was loved. Something I hadn't felt in a very, very long time.

Counting the change took much longer than I anticipated—and half a box of Kleenex. It totaled $193.64. This could pay my grocery bill for three months or my phone bill for half a year. But the real gift—the real gift is the love. It's in knowing that I am not facing the challenges of the world completely alone, because somewhere out there someone is putting their change in a jar.

—*Rachel Storm*

I AM OLD AND HANDICAPPED

Duncan, Oklahoma

Last night there was a loud knock on the door. It was dark. I am old and handicapped. I don't live in the best neighborhood and I am afraid to answer the door after dark. I went to the door and peeked out the window and saw no one. I turned on the porch light and timidly went outside. There, sitting on my porch, was a jar and a book. I had never heard the Christmas Jar story.

I turned over the book and read the back, then yelled into the darkness, "THANK YOU!" as loud as I could. I have damaged vocal cords, so I am sure it wasn't very loud, but it was as loud as I could make it.

I came back inside, sat down in my chair, and cried. It's been a really rough year. Last week I had another mini-stroke right before church. It has been cold here and the furnace won't work right. The cold makes the bones I broke in the accident hurt.

My children can't come for Christmas this year and I will be alone—again. I didn't even feel like putting up my tree. And then out of nowhere came the Christmas Jar. It made me realize how wonderful people are here in Duncan and how I am so blessed to live here and be surrounded by such wonderful people.

I am putting up my tree today.

I found a peanut butter jar from under the sink and put in my first quarter.

—Cheryl

HE PANICKED

Edinburg, Virginia

This year was not our first Christmas Jar experience but it was definitely the most memorable!

A family was suggested that might need a little boost, and even though we didn't know them very well we trusted our friends who said that the jar might be the most important thing they would get this whole year.

We had a hard time finding the house at first because our GPS tried to send us to some neighborhood in Australia. Yes—Australia!

So after a few phone calls we got the right address and were happy to see that we would not be getting a plane to deliver our Christmas Jar.

Everyone but the driver wanted to come up to

the door. It also took a little while to find the family's apartment number. We were a little alarmed to find it on the second floor and spent more time than we probably should have spent figuring out our escape.

We put the jar down and got a head start as one of the kids knocked on the door and ran.

One of my kids went the wrong way down the street and then one of the family's kids was down the stairs and out into the middle of the street shouting, "I see him, I see him!"

My kid crossed the street and tried to be invisible but by then the tears were already flowing hard.

He panicked on where he was supposed to go and rather than wait at the pickup spot he came back down the street looking for our car which was slowed down by being caught in the mud and then having to turn around in a very tight area behind another building.

Meanwhile, our dog, which we had brought along, was barking at someone's cat, only adding to the commotion.

When our last person finally got back to the car

he was almost in hysterics and said, "Well, I'm never doing *that* again!"

We got the detailed play-by-play and promised that no one had been recognized and that we were safe. By the time we all got home, everyone was laughing about our crazy adventure, and even the grouchy one said it was all worth it and we would definitely be doing it again next year.

That's the amazing thing about the Christmas Jar. It's contagious! We all hope the family had a brighter Christmas.

—*Tyrone Maxwell*

LAST YEAR WAS VERY TRYING

Meridian, Idaho

The last year has been very trying for my family. My wife has a disease that affects her muscles and often leaves her in a wheelchair, which makes caring for our children difficult. We are fortunate that I have a job with good insurance. But deductibles and a mountain of debt have made this Christmas very tight. I was really concerned about having enough to get gifts for the kids this year.

Tonight a very loud, quick knock left us finding a jar and a book on our doorstep. The money in the jar will go a long way to making ends meet. Thank you to all who see a need and do what you can. I hope my family can do a jar for a family next year.

—*Tyler*

IN MEMORY OF OUR SON

Powell, Wyoming

I would like to remain anonymous; we live in a very small town and don't want to be found out. Our son passed away a few years ago in December. We were reading the *Christmas Jars* book together as a family. We didn't get to finish it before he passed away, but shortly after he passed away and we finished the book, I started thinking: I didn't want that day in December to be a really sad day for the rest of our lives, so I decided to start the Christmas Jar tradition in our family. We saved our change for the next year. On the anniversary of our son's death, the entire family got together, ate our son's favorite foods, remembered wonderful stories about him, and counted six jars. Then we all went out and anonymously delivered them. It was a great night of shared memories and service to others. I'm sure my son approves of what we did. We immediately started saving for the next year. This year we all got together again and did the same thing. Only we had saved several more jars and we decorated them. I am so happy to have a positive activity for a night that could otherwise be very sad. Thanks for the book and the inspiration.

—*Anonymous*

I FOUND A JAR AND BOOK
ON MY STEP

Waukesha, Wisconsin

My husband was recently diagnosed with terminal colorectal cancer, a large and very aggressive tumor. We brought him home after a three-week stay from the hospital with in-home hospice care.

He had been home for five days and I was having a day of crying. It was a little past 7:30 P.M. when a knock came at my front door. I found no one there but a jar and book on my step.

It brought me to more tears just to know that someone would do that for my family, and to whoever the angel was that delivered it, I just want to let you know that it really meant a lot to know there are still good people in this world and to say THANK YOU!

—*Diane Cummings*

THE CHRISTMAS JAR
IS ABOUT HOPE

Tacoma, Washington

We received a Christmas Jar two years ago. I wrote about it then, but somehow never managed to post this until now. Since that time, my family has walked through even tougher times, only to see God provide in bigger and truly miraculous ways. The biggest miracle was this last March when my husband's heart stopped while we were on a walk. Paramedics revived him, but doctors couldn't figure out the issue, and he wouldn't come out of a coma. With hundreds of people praying, we knew God was with us, no matter the outcome. Today, my husband is fully recovered, to the amazement of every doctor and nurse who aided him during his month-long stay in the hospital. I fully believe that our Christmas Jar experiences of the past years helped plant the seeds of trust that God knows how to find us in every dark and hopeless situation.

The original experience, 2013:

The other night we came home from a school basketball game to find two jars filled with coins sitting on the box next to our front door.

"What are these?" Mike asked.

Then we looked at each other. "Christmas Jars!" Oh, my . . . Christmas Jars!

It was just a year ago Thanksgiving weekend that we learned about Christmas Jars. Randomly, I had picked up a book bearing this title from a sale table at Barnes and Noble. I had never heard of the author, but the thin little book caught my attention as something my mom would like. The best part—it was short enough that she wouldn't disappear from us for too long to read it. And, loving Christmas stories, I picked up a second copy for me.

As predicted, Mom vanished into her bedroom and didn't come out for about four hours, with the book finished. "You have to read this. You will love it." Tears were in her eyes, but she would tell me no more.

Mike and I had a six-hour drive home, and it took only the first chapter to become engrossed. About the time we hit Snoqualmie Pass, we too were wiping away tears. The charm of a story of generosity and hope struck a chord deep within us. I was so moved by the story that I read it to all six of my classes last year. "I'm going to start one of those," I heard more than one student say.

At the time, I pictured myself making a yearly tradition of reading this book to students, but as each school year takes on its own flavor, I didn't know how to squeeze it in this time. One of my seniors did ask me if they could hear *Christmas Jars* again. "We'll see," I told her. I tried to start it with one class, but we only got to the first chapter. My sole success with sharing the story was to send the book to college with my daughter. "Great story, Mom," she wrote in a text soon thereafter.

So now, here I am a year later with two mystery jars brimming with quarters, dimes, a few nickels, and even a $20 bill. Not jars that we prepared for others, but ones meant for us. Humbling. Stunning. Emotional.

So many thoughts went through my head as the meanings of these two jars soaked in. Was it one of my students? Had someone—for a full year—planned this? They knew snatches of the transition we've experienced the last few years, with the closing of Mike's business and his decision to go back to school at fifty years old, starting a whole new career. They knew this, but they couldn't know how uncertain we've continued to be during this time, uncertain how bills were going to be paid, uncertain of the future, uncertain if we are hearing the Lord correctly anymore, uncertain as to why things have gone so very differently than we planned, uncertain how to share with others out of fear of being misunderstood and judged, uncertain how we were going to make the unexpected work out, let alone things like Christmas. Uncertain, and, more honestly, anxious—BUT also slowly becoming impressed that God is closely involved in our journey, and He has us covered.

So, if it was one of the kids—how generous, how perceptive, how much like Jesus, how loved and hopeful they have made me feel.

What if it wasn't one of them? Maybe someone at church? A neighbor? A stranger? Each prospect equally amazing. I can't think of anyone outside of school or my family who knows how impacting the story of the Christmas Jars was to Mike and me last year. So, whoever dropped them off, they were a messenger directly from my Heavenly Father, reminding me that He has everything under control and that I worry FAR TOO MUCH about stuff that will one day fade away.

It's hard to explain the journey we've been on these last few years, but in this long, long season the Lord has brought us to a day-to-day existence where no matter what we've tried to do, He's allowed us just enough for the month at hand. I've called it our "Manna Season." Prone to be planners, always finding it easier to be givers than receivers, this is a scary place to be. Yet, week after week, month after month, God has provided for us in the most amazing, always unexpected ways. Job offers came with extra salary. An unexpected bonus. Unexpected part-time work. An opportunity to go back to school and to start over. Forgotten money in a pocket. Repair help that we didn't have to pay for.

Trades with friends. Extra funds at a moment when we wanted to give to someone else. Twice I have found $20 bills in my wallet when I could have sworn nothing was there earlier. On and on the provisions have come.

There has been an echoing chain of closed doors the last few years. Lots of things lost to us, taken away—more of that uncertainty. Fear. Worry. Even guilt, because even though our journey has included much loss, our loss hasn't been that of close loved ones (at least not recently). Nevertheless, we find ourselves mourning and struggling to understand the future. Guilt because even in the midst of the provisions, I start worrying all over again because the future is made up of a path that is completely invisible to me.

Then . . . the Christmas Jars—an undeniable reminder and a summation of all that God has been doing for us this last year.

I woke up this morning wondering what it is, fully, that the Lord is saying to us through the jars. Even though there are any number of things that we could do with the money, the needs suddenly seem to evaporate. God is so close, continually doing won-drous, unexpected things. We find ourselves thinking of others who need that same message and how we might share some of the hope of our jars with them. And that is really what the Christmas Jar is about: hope, a reminder that God always has and always will take care of that which concerns me. And that He is always close at hand. Immanuel—God with us.

—Shelly Ausmus

I LOST THE MOST SPECIAL PERSON IN THE WORLD

Salina, Colorado

I knew nothing of these jars and the lovely stories until Christmas Eve. Someone left me and my husband two jars and your book.

Ten days ago I lost the most special person in the world: my twin sister. She was a person that the world will miss as much as I will. She had a smile that lit up the world, her friends, and everyone that met her. As twins, we used to joke that she was the butterfly and I was the bee.

For the last two years, I was so lucky to have the support of my husband to leave my own job and family and travel across the country to be with my twin seventeen times! This allowed me to see her and to spend precious time with her and to not have any regrets.

All of this was going on as we were recovering from a very hard few years. My husband lost his job; I was in a horrible accident; I was diagnosed with cancer; and we were in a horrible mudslide and a devastating flood disaster that almost killed me, my husband, and our pets.

Life throws a lot of twists and turns. I think they all lead us to follow a better path or journey in life and to have a better understanding of what others are enduring.

I learned how important it is to live in the present and to accept help from others as well as to give as much as possible.

I will start my own jar. I will pass this along to someone in need.

—Michelle

WE CAN'T BEGIN
TO EXPRESS OUR LOVE

North Ogden, Utah

My husband is a teacher in the LDS Church's seminary and loves his students and is loved by them. Just after school started, the headaches he had been experiencing for a long time suddenly escalated and became unbearable. It was discovered he had blood and fluid on the brain. After waiting for it to be reabsorbed, he finally had surgery to drain and release the pressure. He was in the hospital for most of a month and is now recovering at home, but still even a shower exhausts him. The doctors have said this is akin to having a stroke and will take time to heal. His students and former students are all so wonderful and have done many things to cheer him up. He so wants to be back and they so much want him back. Time will tell if and when that will happen.

Last Sunday night, we heard a knock on our door, and when I answered it, no one was there. Then, some time later, we again heard a knock on the door and this time, when I answered it, there was a huge (I mean HUGE) jar on our front step. It took a lot of work to get it inside, because I couldn't lift it. I weighed the four bowls I had filled with the coins and cash and it all totaled up to about 80 pounds! No wonder I couldn't lift it. This is such a wonderful thing that will help pay the bills that are still coming in and help with physical therapy. We can't begin to express our love and thanks for this act.

Thank you, Jason, for this wonderful idea that is spreading around the nation. I had just read your *Christmas Jars* books, and just this morning finished reading *The 13th Day of Christmas*. I want to rededicate myself to our Savior every day. I love Him so much! Thank you!

—*Valerie Cullison*

THIS ACT HAS GIVEN US HOPE

St. Joseph, Minnesota

This past year, our family has been through one of the most difficult years ever. First, our daughter was diagnosed with a life-threatening illness. In the midst of it, I lost my job. While I eventually found work, it hasn't been enough to provide for our family.

On Thursday, I spent an hour in specific prayer—at Eucharistic adoration—praying that God would provide some sign of hope. I felt very near despair.

So, you can imagine our surprise at finding our first Christmas Jar on our deck last evening—a day after praying. The large jar had the initials *C. J.* (Christmas Jar) written on it.

We are filled with joy and hope and are in disbelief at some anonymous person's/family's generosity, and how God provided during a particularly difficult week when we most needed it.

The jar had a little note on the top of it. We immediately prayed as a family, in thanksgiving for the gift, and prayed for the intentions of those who had so generously given to us.

I cannot explain the hope that this act has given all of us. God is so very good, and acts through each of us. To whoever left us the jar, please know of our gratitude and prayers.

—*Tim and Mary Drake*

FOUR CHRISTMAS JARS
ON MY BACK DOORSTEP

St. Francisville, Louisiana

My kids and I had left the house on Christmas Eve to attend the 7:30 P.M. church service. When we returned there were four Christmas Jars left on my back doorstep filled with nickels, quarters, dimes, dollar coins, and bills. I am a single parent raising my two children and lost my mother to cancer in April of this year. My children are my inspiration and we have grown very close since my separation from their father. One is in college, the other a junior in high school. We weren't planning anything special for Christmas and they knew we weren't going to have an extravagant one spending more than I could afford. When we arrived home and found the jars we were astounded. We wondered who would have done such a deed. My children immediately began thinking of how they would begin their own jars to save throughout the year and had begun thinking of who they wanted to share them with. The conversations we've had since the receipt of the jars have been wonderful and has proven to be a real inspiration.

—*Ada Lord*

I GET TEARS
EVERY TIME I THINK OF IT

Wichita, Kansas

I was sitting in my chair playing a game on my computer, watching my daughter sleep. She didn't feel well and fell asleep on the couch. My son was in his room going through his closet getting out the clothes that are too small. It was silent in my house, not a common thing.

Someone knocked on my door, my dogs started barking, and I got up to answer the door. By the time I got the dogs back and opened the door, I saw a shadow running across the street. She got into a big truck and drove away quickly. I looked down to find a gift bag; inside the bag there was a card addressed to me and my children, a book, and a jar with a big red ribbon.

Completely caught off guard, I brought it all inside and opened it up. There was an unsigned card, the book *Christmas Jars*, and the jar full of money—$348.30, to be exact. All I could do was cry.

I am so overwhelmed that I get tears every time I think of it. How generous of someone to give me a jar full of cash.

My story: I am a single mom. I have been divorced for about seven years now. Last January I started nursing school and my work hours got cut back to twenty-four hours a week due to my clinical rotation. On December 17, 2014, I will receive my LPN pin. In January I take the state board exam and I will officially be a nurse! It has been a rough year and I am very thankful for all of the support I have. My plan is to further my education and get my bachelor's degree and be a traveling nurse.

I can't even begin to describe the gratitude I am feeling right at this moment. I don't know who left me this jar, but I am so blessed that you thought of me and my children.

I look forward to continuing this tradition. It may

not be for a year or two, but I look forward to helping someone in need as they have helped me.

I have already read over half the book. I am thankful for the money, but my restored faith in mankind is what is truly the blessing. It is so nice to know that there are good people left in the world. It makes it easier for me to move forward in my path and keep the tradition of the Christmas Jars going.

Again, thank you to my angel, and may God bless you.

Merry Christmas!

—*Dayla*

AN OVERWHELMING FEELING
OF LOVE, PEACE, AND JOY

Port Jervis, New York

On August 2, 2011, our youngest son, Nick, was in a diving accident and broke his neck. He is paralyzed from the chest down. At twenty-one years old he is having a very difficult time, as is the rest of my family. He was released from rehab right before Thanksgiving, and, needless to say, it was very hard to be thankful for anything. My husband and I were not looking forward to Christmas this year. We have always loved the holiday. But this year there wasn't much to celebrate. We took one day at a time and tried to focus on keeping our son strong and believing in our faith to get us through. At times though, it was very difficult. It was hard on my husband and me to see our son suffering like this.

Then a couple of weeks before Christmas we got a knock at the door. My husband opened the door to see two Santas standing on our porch. They handed him a gift bag which he almost dropped because it was so heavy. I heard the commotion from the other room and ran to the door only to see a group of about eight Santas standing on the sidewalk in front of the house. I went outside to see who they were and they wished my family a Merry Christmas and left as fast as they showed up. My husband and I stood there in shock trying to figure out what had just happened. We opened the bag to find a jar full of coins, bills, and gift cards with a book titled *Christmas Jars*.

I can't describe the overwhelming feeling of love, peace, and joy we both felt that night. It reinforced our faith in God. There are so many good, caring, and kind people in this world. We brought the jar in to show Nick and he smiled. I know he felt so happy knowing there were people out there that really cared. Christmas was good in our house this year. I know next year we will have lots more to be thankful for. The jar is in our room. We've explained to my family what happened to us that night and how it made us feel. We will be doing the same next year for someone else, just as the secret Santas did for us that night. God bless you all and thanks from the bottom of our hearts.

—*Kathy Moscatiello*

LONELY AT CHRISTMAS EVE

Craig, Colorado

I went to our Christmas Eve service at Church and felt very lonely. I came home and started crying. The Lord told me, "You are not alone."

I woke this morning, opened the front door (very rare occasion at this time of morning), and found this jar on my door. This was the gift of Jesus Christ using one of His special children to show me I'm not alone!

—Deborah

SOMEONE MUST
LOVE YOU VERY MUCH

Danville, Illinois

At the end of May 2013, I lost my teaching job due to budget cuts. I was unable to get a teaching job for that fall, but I was able to collect unemployment. Just before Christmas, I found out that I would no longer receive unemployment because the extension of benefits was not included in the federal budget. This put a lot of pressure on my husband, who was in a commission-only paying job.

In mid-August 2014, the pressure was just too great, and he was let go from his job. The pressure had also caused my husband to have medical issues which caused him to be hospitalized for a week in November. Thankfully, he has been able to get unemployment during this time, and I am working for a friend part-time, but we are still struggling.

However, last night, December 3, 2014, we came home from church to find a box sitting on our front steps. I had a hard time lifting it, so I asked my husband to help. My son Ethan, who is four, was very excited to begin opening the gift. In the box was a gift bag filled with all sorts of treats for him: two activity books, two candy-filled candy canes, a box of candy canes, a reading book, and a paper bag that was very heavy.

We opened the paper bag to find a gallon-sized pickle jar filled with change, the book *Christmas Jars*, and a gift card for a local gas station.

I cried as I looked at what God had laid on someone's heart and mind to give us. I took the jar to the bank this morning where the teller thought I was just bringing in shopping money. I was able to share the story with her, two other tellers, and the manager. They had chills as I shared the story. The first teller put the change into the counter. A few seconds later, she came back with three more gift cards and a roll of cash.

Her words to me were, "Someone must love you very much."

I cried again, and even as I sit here at work, typing my story, I am crying. I am also excited to see what we are able to give to someone else next year.

We have been blessed beyond measure, and "thank you" seems so inadequate.

—*Rachel Rice*

A LIST OF EVERYONE
WHO NEEDED SOME JOY

Shiremanstown, Pennsylvania

Last night my family gave away its second set of Christmas Jars. My soul has been touched in ways I never would have thought possible. Our Christmas Jars were meant to bless the lives of others, but it is truly our lives that have been blessed.

The Lord has been good to my family this year. We welcomed the birth of a third grandchild and are currently waiting patiently for the fourth to arrive, we are all healthy, my husband is employed, and I am doing well in school. Yes, life has been kind to us this year, but sadly those we love, know, work with, and who are our neighbors have experienced an untold number of struggles. No, life has not been easy for many of the people that we know.

Deciding who should receive our Christmas Jar this year was proving to be a difficult decision because we know too many people who could use it. So how does one choose which of their friends, co-workers, or neighbors should receive the Christmas Jar? We couldn't choose . . . we simply could not bless one while another struggled this year.

In March of this year my family received a wonderful financial blessing. Not having any plans for the money, we put it in the bank for a rainy day.

Last Monday, I sat down at my desk and made a list of all the people I know who needed some Christmas joy. When I finished, there were twelve families on my list. After making my list, I dumped the contents of the Christmas jar on the table and began counting the change and bills: $439.50. Divided by twelve, that would be about $36.50 per family. Surely we could do better than that, right?

I have always been of the opinion that money is important when you need it, but that we shouldn't focus on having so much of it. Too much of anything is never a good thing.

My husband and I decided that while we may have been financially blessed in March we were really only the safekeepers of that money. We finally understood that the money we received wasn't intended for our personal use. The Lord had other plans for it; we just needed to figure out what those plans were. We figured it out. The money was meant to go to those twelve families, so we withdrew the money from the bank, split it twelve ways, and made our jars. Each family will surely have a wonderful Christmas, but more than having a Happy Christmas, I hoped that they would feel all the love that God has for them.

As for me and my husband, we were overcome with emotion yesterday and completely fell apart. (In a good way.) When one of the jar recipients called on the phone last night to tell us what they found on their doorstep, my heart exploded with joy when they stated, "We feel so loved." They are!

—Anonymous

OUR DOORSTEP WAS COVERED WITH CHRISTMAS JARS

Friendswood, Texas

After twenty-one years of marriage and four of the best blessings in the world, the most important man in our life passed away November 29, 2010. After an overwhelming show of support from friends, family, and the community, we were left to face our first Christmas without our dad and husband.

As per tradition we left to go to our grandparents' for Christmas Eve, a difficult evening to face, but we went in with our heads held as high as possible. After leaving early and in a heartbroken state of mind, we pulled into our driveway to find a path of candles leading to the front door. The doorway was lit up with red and green lights, and our doorstep was covered with over eighty Christmas Jars—all filled with hope, love, and faith.

The jars kept arriving until two A.M. After bringing them all in, my four children and I read the meaning from the book *Christmas Jars* and opened the jars one at a time, sharing verses, notes, and kind words from all the different jars. Our hearts were filled with warmth during what seemed to be such a hard time.

We were not only touched by the notes, but also by the countless gift cards, coins, cash, candy, and food. Most of all though, we were amazed at how what will probably be the saddest Christmas for our family will also be the most memorable—memorable because God poured his love on to our family and wrapped us with thoughts and prayers that were so overwhelming they actually lifted our spirits. We thank each and every Christmas Jar angel that stopped by our house, because they saw a need and chose to serve. May God bless each and every one of them. We know our dad is smiling from above.

—*The Thornhill Family*

SERVING OUR NEIGHBOR

Kingston, Washington

Last year a group of my friends and I read this book and were so inspired that each of us started saving our coins. All year we kept our eye out for someone within our community that we could bless.

We really wanted the jar to go to a stranger so that this act couldn't lead back to us in any way, but living in such a small town, it was proving to be difficult. We felt that it being anonymous was very important. We didn't want recognition or thanks—that defeats the entire purpose of giving selflessly.

Finally, one of us heard a story of a woman who had been diagnosed with uterine cancer. This woman was going to have to have a hysterectomy, her house was being foreclosed on, and her teen daughter was pregnant.

It seemed that life just kept hitting her with one thing after another. She is also known in our community as someone who helps others and is always putting people before herself.

We found out where she lived (benefits of a small community) and went to deliver the jar. At first we set it at the end of her walkway, banged on the side of her house and made a run for it. We waited a minute and then drove around the block to make sure it had been picked up. It was a *very* stormy night and we didn't want the jar to fill with water or get stolen.

This woman had a huge septic truck parked in front of her house so I parked on the opposite side of it and turned off all of my lights. It was dark out so she couldn't see that someone was there, but we could peek between the cab of the truck and the septic tank and watch her.

We sent one of the girls back down to the jar to move it in front of the door and knock. She almost lost her flip-flop in the mad dash back to the car, but she was safely inside before a man came to the door and found the jar. I don't think he knew what it was because he picked up the copy of the book we had left, looked at it, and tossed it to the floor before trying to pick up the jar. The jar was way heavy and felt like it was filled with cement so when he couldn't lift the jar he went back into the house and closed the door, obviously not knowing it was money and probably thinking it was some prank by a neighbor kid.

Then the woman came out and found the book. She looked around very confused and then went to pick up the jar. You could see when she realized what it was because she looked shocked and even more confused, looking everywhere for who could have left this. She had no idea why there was money on her porch or what exactly a Christmas Jar was. She started to walk down her walkway, so we panicked and sped away, not wanting her to see us.

The blessing of Facebook is that we were able to find her page and read what she had written about the jar. She posted asking what it was and thanking profusely whoever did this. She said she was crying and couldn't believe it, that at first they didn't know if they should call the cops or if it was someone wanting a donation. She couldn't believe that it was really for her. Reading through the posts and seeing how touched she was is all the thanks we could ever want. So many people commented on her post—over eighty people in a few short hours, many of them saying they too wanted to now do a jar. Random acts of kindness really do spread like wildfire. One person does one thing and then others want to do good—it spreads and spreads, infecting everyone with happiness and the urge to pay it forward.

None of us have ever been so filled with laughter and joy. Blessing another person, giving so much money (over $300) to someone anonymously, was amazing, and I plan to do it every year—I think we all do.

—Chelsea